ACCIDENTALLY NOAH

CAINE & GRACO SAGA BOOK 1

E.M. SHUE

ACCIDENTALLY
NOAH

Cover Design by Leah Holt of Always Ink Covers

Editing by Nadine Winningham of The Editing Maven

www.authoremshue.com

emshue@authoremshue.com

❀ Created with Vellum

For my girls.
Always and forever, no matter where you go or what you do, I
will love you.

PROLOGUE

I sit in my car several houses down the street watching her parents' house. I'm so glad I overheard the conversation in the store between her mom and another woman. Of course, she didn't know I was there, hiding around the corner. I'm not supposed to be anywhere near them, but I must get her back. I need her.

My skin crawls in anticipation. It's been over five years since I've seen her. The night she left me, she broke me, but I always knew she would come back to me. She is my queen. I've killed for her. She doesn't know it, but I killed the boy who took her virginity and her away from me.

The yellow cab pulls up in front and sits there for a moment. I slide down in my seat so she can't see me and watch as the back door opens. The dark cap on my head covers my blond hair.

"Hey, you're not supposed to be here." The old, nosey neighbor beats on the top of my car. "You better leave before I call the cops."

"Leave me alone, you fucking bat." I sit up and yell at her.

I'm about to pull out my gun when movement in front of me catches my eye.

I watch her move to the side to talk to the cabbie. She's beautiful. From this distance I can see the sun-kissed glow of her skin, like she's spent time out in the sun. She's in distressed skinny jeans that hug all her curves and are rolled at the cuffs showing her ankles. A white T-shirt with a black suit jacket over the top. Over her arm is another coat and her bag. The high-heeled black strappy type of shoes would have to go. I don't like how provocative the outfit is, but I can see she's matured in her style. Her blond hair is long down her back and straightened. It shines in the November sun.

The woman continues to yell as I watch my queen stand on the sidewalk trying to decide if she's going to go in. Instead she turns and looks my way. I know the moment she sees me, and her fear is evident by the tightening of her body.

"Yeah, babe, you owe me something," I say to the empty car.

She turns away shaking herself as I turn over the engine ready to go to her or take off. She'll decide what my decision will be. She has this one chance to prove she still wants me or not.

She looks up at her parents standing on the porch. Her mother has her hands over her mouth and her father looks thinner than he used to. She turns back to look at me and points. I put the car in drive as both her brothers push past their parents and come off the porch. I whip the car around and watch them chase after me in the rearview mirror. The last glimpse I have of her is her jumping back into the cab and taking off in the opposite direction.

Fuck, wrong decision, my queen. Now I'm going to play dirty.

That old lady messed up my plans. She'll be taken care of. Then I'm going to find my queen and make her mine again. Five and a half years is too long to be without her sweetness. I've sacrificed too much for her and done too much.

CHAPTER ONE

KENZIE

"**K**eni, why did you leave the party so quickly on Saturday?" Trina asks as I sit down and start the tedious process of logging onto all the systems I need to work.

"What do you mean? I stayed for a couple of hours." I hate parties and socializing.

"Yeah, only a couple hours, girl. How am I supposed to marry you off if you're not out partying?" My best friend raises a single perfectly shaped eyebrow.

Trina's long brown hair is pulled up in a bun. Her makeup is on point from her red lips to her longer fingernails. Her Puerto Rican heritage gives her the perfect sienna complexion; meanwhile, I'm losing my tan I've loved having for the last few years. We are complete opposites, but as soon as we met, she basically said we were going to be best friends. She's the girly girl and I'm the tomboy. Trina likes to party and have fun with her husband. I'm a homebody. I like my romance novels, bubble baths, and plants.

"I don't want to get married. Besides, I haven't found the right guy to even take a ride with." We both laugh because that's one of the problems she's had with me since we met in training.

She took me under her wing and has tried to fix me up with every man she knows, even my old friends back in Hawaii did the same thing. Everyone seems to think because I'm not in a relationship that means I'm lonely. Shoot, I have all my book boyfriends, and they don't let you down like real men tend to do. They don't have insecurities about height, they just want to protect and love you.

Before either of us can respond, our phones ring, and our shift kicks into full swing. We work in the nation's busiest dispatch center. Trina still floats between fire and police, while I'm exclusive to police dispatch. Today both of us are on police. I'm working Lower Manhattan and she's working the Upper East Side.

"Dispatch, 1506."

"Dispatch." I acknowledge I'm listening to him.

"10-84." Unit 1506 from the 1st Precinct lets me know they've arrived on the scene of a body discovered in Battery Park. The voice is husky and sexy sounding. Sex on a mic.

"On Scene at 1300." I enter the information into the system.

As the day progresses, I'm feeling fried and feel the tingles of a headache forming. I'm not sleeping very well again. I knew moving back here would cause the memories to come back, the nightmares, I just never expected them to start so soon. I thought I was stronger and could avoid them.

I work four ten-hour shifts as I'm prepping to be a trainer, and with all my prior experience, they couldn't pass up on it. Trina is completely new to dispatching, so she only works eights and is getting ready to leave for the day.

"Russo, you're on holdover," my supervisor states from right behind me.

I drop my head, that's another automatic five hours on shift. I hate holdovers but know they are a part of this job. If someone gets sick, I'm held on to cover half their shift and the next person is called in early, or someone else comes in. Dispatching in New York is busier than in Honolulu, but I enjoy it.

"A little notice would have been nice." I look up at him with a smile and he shrugs as he walks away. I know he gets as much notice as I do.

As a trainer in training, this is part of what must be done to prove I'm ready to teach others what I know and how to work this job.

"Dispatch, 1506." The sexy voice comes across the line again.

Man, I'm going to fantasize about that voice tonight. I smile.

"Dispatch."

"10-85. District 62." The sexy voice requests additional units from the 62nd Precinct and I pray everyone is safe.

"Location?"

He rattles off an address I know, and my fingers tremble as I type in the information, trying not to let the panic take over. I knew the family that used to live there, and I know one of the family members still does. I grew up in Bensonhurst. That address is just down the road from my parents' house. They still live in the house I grew up in.

"10-10. Shots fired," another voice, not the sexy honeyed voice, says; he must be the partner.

"Copy," I answer, and key in the info before transferring the call to the dispatcher for the 62nd Precinct.

I stay on the line to help if necessary and make sure my

unit is okay. The dispatcher calls out for additional units and sends ambulance to the area. I stay on until I hear the all clear for my unit, and say a silent prayer that Mr. Sexy Voice is okay and that it isn't anyone I know, or knew.

By the time my shift is over all the trains have run, so I'll have to take a cab home. I moved to the Bronx hoping to get assigned to the new location there, but I ended up taking the Brooklyn position because of the trainer opportunity and the extra pay. It means I'll be looking for a place closer to work when I have the money saved up. I like my little studio apartment in the Bronx, but it's nothing like the place I had in Hawaii. I shared a small house with a friend of mine and her daughter. We met one day at the gym and just like Trina, she decided she needed to be my friend.

Now every second I'm in Brooklyn is another second my past could come back to find me, but I couldn't stay away from my family any longer. A living nightmare could start again, and this time it would be worse because I broke the rules. I defied him.

I head out into the cool May night and shiver. I miss living in the warm tropics of Hawaii, but it was time for me to come home. I tried to stay away from people and be on my own, but they wouldn't let me. Plus, as a dispatcher, you get close to the people you work with due to the stress levels. I've gotten several texts from my friends asking how I'm doing and if I'm really not going back. I want to go back, but it was time for me to pull up my big girl panties and take responsibility for my actions as a dumb teenager. I'm grown up enough now and I learned a lot while I was in Hawaii about accepting the mistakes I made, and being able to overcome them.

I hail a cab and give him my address knowing a trip to

the Bronx is going to dip into my precious meager savings. It took everything I had to move back here and to pay the deposits on my new apartment.

When I step into my apartment, I text Trina to let her know I made it home. She has taken the roll as the big sister almost too far. She doesn't know I have two older brothers who were so overprotective that guys couldn't even call the house without them going crazy. That's what I got for being the first female Russo born in four generations. Her response is quick and makes me smile.

Trina: We will finish our discussion tomorrow.

She just won't give up. She doesn't like that I come home to an empty apartment, or that I'd rather bury myself in a romance novel, or listen to music than socialize. I connect my phone to an external speaker and start up my favorite Spotify playlist. I don't miss all the island music or the reggae. I like my soulful songs, rock and dark music. Maybe it's my past but I still like it. Give me some Halestorm, Ruelle, or Halsey any day.

I pull my long blond hair down from the bun and slip out of my work uniform and into a pair of boxers and a tank top. Dinner for one consists of a grilled ham and cheese sandwich and a glass of water. After that I walk around performing my Monday night weekly ritual of checking all my plants. It took me months to find all the ones I wanted and now my apartment is practically a jungle. I practice some yoga and stretches to relax myself, hoping I'll be able to sleep.

A ping from my laptop alerts me I have a message. I check my email and sure enough I have a message on the board for lost loved ones.

MarcBrooklynboy: KenFlower, we need to talk.

Shit. I don't want to post too much information but I have no choice. What if Papa is sick again?

KenFlower: RE:MarcBrooklynboy same number?

He responds right away with a yes.

I log off the board and disconnect my cell phone. I can't call him because if I hear his voice I'll cave and give in. The desire to see my family is so great. I almost gave in and stayed the last time I saw them. If I wasn't afraid my presence would get them hurt I would've stayed. But the voice in my head still tells me they are in danger and he will hurt them.

Keni: What's up? Is Papa okay?

Marco: Yes, he's okay. Are you going to try to come out again? It's been 6 months. Maybe it was a fluke and he won't come around again. I haven't seen him around the neighborhood.

Keni: I can't chance it. The risk is too much. I'll message you soon.

Marco: Come on. Mama cried for days because you left. Is he threatening you? Do we need to call the police? You know Zo and I will take care of him for you.

Keni: I'm doing what's best. Please tell her I love her and it's not her fault. I made the mistakes, not them. I can't discuss it. You and Zo don't need to get into trouble for me. You've already given up so much for me. I love you but I need to go. Bye.

Marco: Love you, sissy. I never gave up what I didn't want to.

That's the problem, I made the wrong choices. I let a man into my life when I was only a child. Now I have to face those consequences.

I climb in bed with my latest romantic suspense book,

and read a chapter before falling asleep to thoughts of the smooth honeyed tones of Mr. Sexy Voice.

I'M careful of all the people around me as I ride multiple trains to get to the dispatch center early the next morning. For years now it's been a habit to be aware of my surroundings and those around me. I can't risk him finding me again. As an added precaution now that I'm back, I ride the wrong trains and double back just to make sure I'm not followed.

I step through the doors of the center and swipe my badge to enter the secure location. I stop at my locker and drop off my purse and cell phone before heading to my post. Cell phones don't work in the control room because it's a virtual dead zone.

"Acosta, you're on fire today," the supervisor advises Trina when she arrives.

I'm in earlier than her today due to an every other week jiu-jitsu class I have. My supervisor thankfully accommodates the schedule for me.

After a couple hours of calls and busy time there is a slight lull.

"Okay, what gives? Gino said you barely fucking talked to him at the party." Trina's Queens accent is coming out strong.

Before I can respond, she holds up a finger to signal she has another call.

"Okay, spill, Keni," she says after she logs a fire crew as back in station.

"I'm sorry, I can't date Gino." I start. How am I going to explain this to her? She's a regular size girl and I'm not. I'm taller than most women.

"Why not? He's fucking perfect for you, Kenzie." She uses my full name.

"He's shorter than me. I don't have a problem with short guys, I just don't date them. I have too much money invested in my heels to give them up. History has taught me that men like Gino have an attitude toward taller women." Honesty is always the best policy. Right?

"So, you have a problem with short man syndrome?" She laughs, her cackle carries and others turn to look at us.

Oh my God, did she just say that? Okay, maybe I do a little bit, but if a shorter guy wanted to date me and didn't have an attitude, I might consider it, but not Gino.

"No, I didn't say that. Some men have that issue and Gino actually is one of those assholes. And just because he's Italian doesn't make him perfect for me." I don't cuss as much as I used to, but it sometimes comes out. My old roommate was a single mom and I didn't want her little girl's first word to be "fuck."

"Oh, you can tell now who is going to have an issue with your height?" She starts to argue with me when the supervisor comes up behind her.

"Acosta, your mic was still on. All of Manhattan Fire heard your conversation before I cut you off."

I blush so hard I physically can feel the burn. Every fire department in Manhattan heard me cut down short men. My supervisor turns to look at me. He's taller, so I know he's not mad at me, just upset the convo went on air.

"I need a break." I jump up and run for the restroom, needing to get away from the embarrassment.

"Wait," Trina hollers for me, but my legs keep me going.

I don't know how to fix this, and I pray no one heard it. I splash water on my face and can't wait for tonight. I have practice at the gym and I really can't wait to beat on a person for a few moments. To physically push my body to the extreme limits.

When I step out of the restroom, Trina looks at me with a slight smile on her face.

"I'm so sorry, Keni," she says, and I nod at her.

She doesn't act sorry. She can't hide the smile and it's like a joke to her.

Of course, my luck is never good. Calls came in for the rest of my shift directed toward me. Some were complaints and suggested I attend sensitivity training, and some wanted to take me out to prove I was wrong about short men. I didn't speak to Trina the rest of my shift, and when I took off afterward, I made sure I was out the door before her.

"Ma'am, I was wondering if you could help me?" A tall man steps up to me as I head down the stairs.

I look up into his piercing blue eyes. His brown hair is a tad long. He stands at least six foot four. And fuck a duck, he's in a station jacket with a Manhattan Fire emblem on it.

I didn't slip my jacket over my polo, so I'm clearly advertising who I work for too.

"Maybe." I step back from him, not wanting to be too close. I'm always conscious of how close people get to me.

"I'm looking for a dispatcher named Keni or Kenzie."

I try to hide my surprise. I'm glad my badge is put away so he doesn't know it's me.

"Why?" I ask him, and bite my bottom lip in worry of what he's going to say.

"I'm Jericho and I want to talk to her." He smiles like he's going to disarm me with it.

White teeth shine, his lips are smooth and full, and he has a five o'clock shadow proving he shaved this morning. He thinks his smile is going to give him whatever he wants. I bet it works on a lot of girls, just not me.

"Let me guess, you heard what she said?" I question him with a bite in my voice.

"Well, yeah." He smiles again, this time dimples show as he starts to laugh. "I was going to see if she wanted to grab a bite with me." He holds out his hand for me to shake but I turn my back on him.

"I don't know her. Goodnight." I take off but I'm not fast enough.

"Keni, wait! I'm so sorry," Trina yells, and now he knows I'm who he's looking for.

He goes to make a grab for my arm but I twist away and hail a cab to take me to the gym.

"You're not my fucking type," I yell as I jump in the cab and flip him off.

If I had more money in my savings I would run again, maybe I would go back to Hawaii. Get away from everyone. Although, I've run before with little to no money. But I'm older and wiser now. At least that's what I keep telling myself. And I've learned not to run from my problems.

Trina: I really am sorry.

Keni: Please just forget it happened. That's what I want to do.

Trina: Will you text me later?

Keni: I have jits tonight

ON TONIGHT's menu is a chef salad I picked up at the local grocer and a glass of white wine from my stash. Two more days of work then I'll be off for three days and rotate to the night shift. I hate that I'm on a flipping schedule right now but it's what I have to suffer through as they prep me to become a trainer. I worked as a dispatcher in Hawaii for the last four and a half years. I was trained by the federal government and worked on one of the military bases. The experience is what NYPD wants for their trainer position. I've also taken extra training through the years.

I forget to text Trina and the next morning she corners me in the locker room.

"Look, Keni, I know what happened yesterday sounded bad to you, but it could be good. I mean, look at that guy from last night."

"Good? How is it good that I'm now known as the fucking girl that judges men on their height? Oh, and calls them assholes."

"Honestly, babe, that's not what you were trying to say. I was teasing you. That guy last night just wanted to talk to you. He was cute, wasn't he? If I didn't have my hubby. Man. Phew, I could teach him some things. Yummy."

"No! I'm sorry, Trina, I can't do this." I swing my hand between the two of us.

If I've done one thing in the last few years, it's push people away before they can really hurt me, or before they get to know who I really am. I don't want to lose any more people when my life goes crazy, because it will. Experience has taught me it will. And I can't let that happen.

If Trina really knew what an awful person I am, she wouldn't want to be my friend. If she knew the choices I've made and how bad I hurt my own family...

She grabs my arm.

"You're not going to push me away, Keni. I've watched you do that to other people, but you and me, we are friends."

"How? We just met six months ago."

"I know. Now I'm sorry. I'll field any more calls and I'll even pretend I'm you if you want me to." She holds both my hands in hers.

I'm so tired of being alone. I miss Lysta and Zoe. I miss other friends I've run from.

"Okay. You don't need to do that, though. I can handle it."

"Good. Let's get today busted out."

The day goes by without any incident and so does the next.

CHAPTER TWO

NOAH

"Hey, Caine, Warren, my office. Now," the captain yells, and I look over at my partner and roll my eyes.

"Coming, sir," Linc calls back. "You did this, buddy, you owe me. My ass can't take any more of you stepping out of line into danger. I have a little girl to think about." He points at me and I groan.

He's right, not only did I put my own life in danger, but his as well, and he has an eleven-year-old little girl.

For the last six months all I can think about is death. Losing my best friend and the woman I thought I would be able to talk into coming back to me has put me on this mission of destruction. I've been left wondering when someone will want to live a life with me. Wondering if I'm ever going to find the one to settle down with. Really wondering if my father was right.

I adjust my tie, tightening it back up. I'll take the ass chewing that's coming our way. I know we should have

17

waited for backup to arrive before we breached the door, or at least called in what we were doing.

I think back to that day. The sexy melodic voice on the radio with the Brooklyn accent had caused my pants to tighten. A reaction I hadn't had in a long time. That was the first shock of the day. The second shock came when we went to question a woman regarding the remains of a murdered teenager, and found the woman dead and the murderer still on the premises. When the first bullet from the perp's gun struck the wall next to where I stood, I knew I was done with my destructive ways. It's time to live. It's time for me to get on with my life. Kat wouldn't have wanted this for me.

"Captain, I was the one who ran headlong in without waiting for backup," I say as soon as we step through the door. "It won't happen again."

"Good job for pointing out your mistakes, Caine, but that's not all we need to discuss. Where is the case now and how does the woman play into it?"

"The victim was the woman's grandson. We're working with homicide over at the 62nd on this one." Linc supplies

"What have you found on the victim so far?"

"Other than he was eighteen years old at time of death, and had just graduated from FDR, nothing else." We've hit a wall.

"Do some more digging, and keep working with the 62nd. Make sure these aren't related."

"Okay, Captain," we both say and head toward the door.

"Caine, stay." The captain stops me, and I turn around. "Don't make me put you on leave. Get your shit together and don't ever pull that crap again. You and Warren have been good for this division since you joined it."

"Yes, sir. It won't happen again."

My phone vibrates in my pocket, and I pull it out. My

brother Jericho's name flashes across the screen and I hit ignore.

"Okay, get out of here and get your ass laid or something." The captain dismisses me and laughs as I walk out.

Laid. There aren't any chicks I'm currently into. Besides, I'm busy getting my house into shape. My dad raised my brothers and me to believe when you found the woman meant for you, you would know it in your bones. Like your soul was singing. To this day I still think he was crazy, but I can't argue with him. He was a New York beat cop killed on 9/11. That's why working at the 1st Precinct is important to me. I work the area my father died in.

My cell phone buzzes again.

"What do you want asshole?" I answer, my voice gruff.

"Well, that's a nice way to answer your phone." Jericho laughs.

"What?"

"Was wondering if you want to go on a blind date?"

"No." I'm not going to let my little brother set me up. Besides, I know his taste in women, and it's not the same as mine. I want someone ready to settle down, not go out and party all the time.

"I didn't date her. I swear."

We don't date each other's exes. Although, both Zeke and Jericho joked often about stealing Kat after we broke up. But who wouldn't want to date a supermodel?

"Still doesn't mean I'm going to date her." I smile into the phone.

"Dude, come on. I'll set it all up. Uncle Romeo's place next week. Friday. She's a beautiful blonde, and tall with long legs. You'll love her. She's feisty too."

"Feisty? Fuck, Jericho, if she's so perfect, why aren't you dating her?" That's the obvious question.

"Well...I did ask her out. She said I wasn't her type. But you could be. Come on, man."

I think about it for a moment. My captain's words replay in my head, and the fact a good dinner at Romano's Little Italy would be nice.

"Well?"

"Okay."

"Awesome. I'll set it all up."

"If this is a trick, I'm fucking you up and throwing you out of my house."

"Man, would I do that to you?" He laughs as he hangs up.

Yes, he would do that, little fucker finds joy in causing me problems.

I sit down at my desk and pore over the case file in front of me. When the victim, Thomas Winthrop, went missing, the last to see him was his grandmother. Now she's dead. Her statement from six years ago mentions an ex-girlfriend who lived a couple houses down. But the girl had run away.

"Hey, coroner has some stuff for us." Linc interrupts my thoughts.

"Yeah, we also have an ex-girlfriend that might know some things. But she ran away from home about the same time our victim disappeared." I inform him. I don't like coincidences.

"Is the name listed?"

"Not that I can see. I'll call the original detectives and see if I can get anything on her."

"Okay. Let's go." He tosses the keys to me and we head out to our car.

He calls in to let dispatch know we are leaving the precinct.

The rest of the day is spent going over evidence with the crime scene unit and the coroner. Winthrop's remains showed signs of trauma before he was killed by a single GSW to the back of the head. The kid was tortured. Several of his fingers were broken, along with both kneecaps and shins. We got lucky on identification. He had his ID on him and we matched his teeth to dental records. Whatever happened to this kid, he deserved to be treated better than dumped under a cement slab in Battery Park. Thank goodness for those city tax dollars at work replacing cracked and damaged cement or who knows how long he would've been under there. Maybe that's the other reason I flew through the door instead of waiting for backup.

WHEN I FINALLY GET TO my brownstone on the Upper East Side, I'm ready to relax. I head up to my large master suite on the second floor and take a quick shower to get the smell of death off me. Afterward I head down to the kitchen to grab my takeout off the counter before making my way to my man cave in the basement.

I take a seat in my favorite leather recliner and flip on the eighty-five-inch TV. My team, the New Jersey Devils, is out, but the New York Rangers are in the final game of the second round of the Eastern Division of the Stanley Cup Playoffs. They are playing the Washington Capitals, my brother Zeke's team.

My phone buzzes across the side table as I'm eating and yelling at the screen.

"Caine." I answer without looking at the display.

"Fucking overtime." Zeke's voice comes across the line.

"Hell yeah, we got you." I laugh as I wait to see what's going to happen.

"Hell no."

"You coming home for Sunday dinner?" I ask him this question every time we talk. He avoids coming home as much as possible. I don't know why but I hope someday he'll tell me.

"Nope. Too busy on this case."

"Yeah, I know what you mean about cases. Ma's not going to be happy."

"Well, I can't change that I work down here."

I don't tell him the obvious, he could come home and we could work in the same department.

"Stop thinking that. I'm happy here," he says, like he read my mind. "How are you holding up?"

"I'm good. Why?" I raise my eyebrow. Zeke doesn't do touchy-feely. He's the surly bitter one of the three of us. Jericho does the comedy, and me, I'm just a loner.

"Well, it's been five months since she was buried and according to Jer, you haven't dated since...well...he said forever." Zeke laughs.

"I'm doing better. Kat wouldn't want me to be hung up on her and would want me to get on with my life. Besides, fucking Jer is setting me up on a blind date." I look at the screen and cheer when the Rangers score. "You lose, fucker, that's a hundred. Ha." I laugh at him. I don't tell him about the near miss from the other night.

"Yeah, fuck you. I'll be up in a couple weeks. I have a meeting with some homicide detectives and FBI up there."

"Dinner?"

"Yeah, Romano's?"

"You're on." I laugh as he hangs up.

I hear the front door open upstairs and wait to see if Jericho's going to come down. He knows not to bring girls to my house anymore after the last one camped out on the steps trying to get his attention. Jer is a love 'em and leave 'em kinda guy. Not that I didn't have my fair share of one-night stands, but I'm getting too old for that shit. I want to settle down. I want a family and someone to come home to other than my brother. I want a wife and babies. I want to see her in my kitchen with her stomach rounded with my child. I know I shouldn't want that but I'm tired of being alone and tired of missing out.

"Hey, did you record it?" Jericho's tall frame ducks down to look at me as he comes down the staircase.

The height of the staircases was one of the only considerations I couldn't change in the house. All of us are tall, but I'm taller by an inch at six foot four. I have them both in mass and weight too. I tend to lift weights when I'm not working on the house or at work. Since I don't have very many other distractions, I work out a lot.

"Yep, but I can save you and tell you." I laugh.

His phone pings. "Too late, Zeke just messaged me." He looks up from his phone. "Fucker ruined it."

"Got held over?"

"Yeah, had a long call."

"So, who is this girl?" I ask, my curiosity getting the better of me.

"She's a friend of a friend. She can tell you about herself. I don't know much. She just moved back here from somewhere out west."

"Okay. Well I'm gonna call it a night. There's leftovers." I nod over my shoulder to the pizza sitting on the bar behind me.

I head up to my room and fall fast asleep.

"How did you know Mama was the one?"

"Son, when you find the girl, you'll feel it in your bones. It's like your soul is singing. She'll be it. When I met your mama, it took me just looking at her."

Dad's voice invades my sleep and I sit up straight. My room is dark, and I look at the clock. It's three in the morning, but I get up and head down to the gym in the basement to work out for a while before going into the office for the day.

CHAPTER THREE

KENZIE

I can't believe I'm actually doing this. When Trina asked me to go out on a date with a friend's brother, I told her no several times. But then she talked me into it. She was right, I couldn't be alone anymore. Besides, it was only one date.

Things have died down a bit since the radio fiasco last week. I still get a few guys trying to ask me out. Thank goodness Trina runs interference so I don't have to deal with them like I did that night with that tall firefighter. I can't remember his name right now.

I'm meeting my date at Romano's Little Italy. I know I'm a little early, but I couldn't help it, blame the train schedule. His name is Noah, and that's all Trina would tell me. The mystery is probably why I'm here more than anything else. That and I can't stand standing someone up. I wouldn't want it done to me.

So here I am in a rose sateen mini blouse dress. I made

sure to grab my raincoat and pocketed my umbrella. It's in the seventies but the weatherman warned we'd get May showers tonight.

I step through the door and the aroma instantly transports me to my mom's kitchen. It's dark and takes my eyes a moment to adjust. When they do, I look around and take in the decor. It's not over the top like the typical cliché Italian restaurants. There are actually large tables in the middle of the room for family style dinners. Another thing I miss.

"Hello, how can I help you?" a beautiful dark-haired woman asks.

She looks like she did a season on *Jersey Shore* with the big hair and overdone eyes. I smile and try not to laugh at her. It sucks that most Americans think this is what Italian-Americans look like. That we go around and say shit like "GTL." My brothers were never about the "gym, tan, laundry" lifestyle, nor have they ever called themselves guidos. I choke on a laugh at the thought.

"I'm here to meet Noah," I say as I compose myself.

"He's not here." She doesn't offer me a table or to wait somewhere, and that's when I see the jealousy.

Oh yeah, she likes Noah, and me being here bothers her. If tonight goes the way my luck usually does, she can have him.

"I'll wait, then." I sit down on the bench and cross my legs, tucking them to the side and against the bench so they don't look so long or make my skirt look shorter or indecent. My thigh tattoo is visible in this outfit.

"*Mi bella*, you're here for Noah." A tall dark-haired man dressed in a tailored black suit and loafers steps from the back and smiles at me.

He's older but still quite handsome with his rugged good

looks and his dark stubble of shadow. His eyes are a deep brown. His hair brushes mid-collar at the back. I can tell he wasn't born here by his strong Italian accent.

"Yes." I smile at him.

"Come this way."

He reaches out his hand and helps me up. In my four-inch heels, I stand at eye level with him. He tucks my hand into the crook of his arm and leads me to the bar.

He pulls out a stool for me to sit and takes my jacket. I take a seat and cross my legs, then twist to the bar.

"How about a glass of the house Chianti?"

"Yes, please." I smile at him and feel like I'm at home.

He stands at the bar and pours the dark liquid, just enough for me to have a taste and nod my approval.

"Tell me, *bellissima,* what's your name?"

"Kenzie Russo."

"I'm Romeo Romano." He holds out his hand, but when I go to shake it, he twists my hand and kisses the back of it.

His name fits him. He's so suave he doesn't even have to try to flirt, it just comes naturally to him. He reminds me of my Uncle Enzo before he died. My oldest brother was named after him.

"How long have you been here?" I wave my hands, indicating the surroundings.

"Oh, we've been here for about fifteen years. How long have you lived here in the city? And where in Italy is your family from?"

"I was born in Brooklyn, but I moved away for several years. Oh, um..." A voice behind me has me turning to the entrance of the bar.

"Holy fuck," the deep husky voice says, and I swallow my tongue.

I'm hoping this is Noah. He stands at about six foot four with dark brown hair cut close to his head but longer on top. His dark brows aren't super thick but enhance his eyes. God, I hope he doesn't go get those done because then it will be a big mark against him. I like a man's man. No metro pretty boys for me. His chin is covered in dark stubble indicating he hasn't shaved yet today, maybe not since yesterday. He isn't just tall, his body is huge. He's in blue slacks with a lighter blue button-down that is open at the collar. The cuffs are rolled up showing large forearms. I start to squirm in my seat.

"There's my nephew now," Romeo says, and I turn to look at him, my hair swinging around my shoulders. I flat ironed it so it's straight and hanging down to mid-back.

NOAH

I step through the door of my uncle's restaurant and ignore the hostess. She's been trying to get in my pants for months now since she was hired. I don't see anyone waiting but then I hear Uncle Romeo from the bar. I step through and stop dead in my tracks.

Sitting on the stool is the most beautiful woman I've ever seen. Long straight blond hair falls down her back. She's in a rose satin like dress short enough I can see the tattoo on her left thigh. She has on open-toed sky high fuck me heels in a pale color. And I can't help the words that come out of my mouth.

"Holy fuck."

She turns to look at me and I feel like I've been punched in the solar plexus. I can't make out her eye color from this distance, but fuck, her lips beg for my kisses. The fuller bottom lip demands I bite it. The image of her mouth wrapped around my cock causes me to have to adjust myself. Thank goodness she misses that when Uncle Romeo announces my arrival.

I walk to her and hold out my hand.

"Noah Caine, you must be Kenzie." I hear the growl in my voice as I take in her fair skin and pale gray eyes.

She takes my hand and the shock of awareness is so strong I know she's mine. She steps down from the stool and in the heels, she stands at six two. I can't wait to feel those long legs wrapped around my body as I take her. I lace my fingers with hers and lead her from the bar toward a table in the back. I don't want to share her with anyone, not even my uncle.

"Wait, my glass." She stops, but Uncle Romeo saves her.

"I got it. Go have a seat, *bella*," he says, and I look back at him. My jaw tightens and I squint my eyes to let him know she's mine. "Loud and clear, Noah." He smiles at me.

The old man would flirt with a nun. But he's not going to flirt with this girl anymore.

I pull out a chair for her and smell tropical flowers floating off her body as she sits and I push her chair in.

"Thank you for having dinner with me tonight," I say as I sit down across from her. Not liking the distance from her, I slide to the side so we are next to each other.

"Thank you too. It's been so long since I've had some good Italian food. I can't wait." She sighs.

I wonder at her statement for all of two seconds until she tips her head to the side and her hair slides toward me. My hands itch to touch it. To wrap my fingers in it and pull her mouth to mine.

"That's a shame and it will be rectified tonight. Tell me a bit about yourself." I watch her closely and see when she starts to close off on me.

I lean in closer to her. "Baby, you can tell me anything you want. You don't have to worry with me." Her lips tip up and again I notice her fuller bottom lip that I want to suck into my mouth.

Before she can say anything, my uncle comes out with tonight's special. He and the server set the plates in front of us and I watch as she takes her first bite.

"Oh God, don't tell my mama this is better than hers," she says around a bite of lasagna.

Her moans make me want to throw her over my shoulder and take her out of here. I want to hear those sounds as I slide between her legs and into her heaven. I know it would be heaven too. Just like I know she is meant to be mine. Always and forever.

"I won't tell yours if you don't tell mine that her brother's is better than hers." I chuckle and she laughs. It's full and causes me to inhale quickly. The more I'm around her the more I want her. The more I know she's meant to be mine.

"I'll start. I grew up in Newark, I'm the middle of three boys. My oldest brother and I followed in our father's footsteps after he was killed on 9/11. I'm a detective with the 1st Precinct."

I watch her body tighten up and this reaction I'm used to. Women usually want to be with a cop for the fun of it or they don't because of the danger. I hope she isn't either of those. I want her to be with me because she's drawn to me, like I'm drawn to her.

"What does your youngest sibling do?" she asks, her voice tight as she reaches for her wine glass.

She swirls the dark blend before putting it to her lips, and I watch it slide into her mouth. I can't look away from the erotic sight. She puts her glass down and reaches for her fork again as she nods for me to continue.

"Oh, Jericho is a firefighter."

She stops eating and puts her fork down.

"You've got to be fucking kidding me." She drops her napkin down next to her and rises. I stand up with her.

"I don't understand. Is something wrong?"

CHAPTER FOUR

KENZIE

My head whips around when he says his brother's name followed by he's a firefighter, and I've had enough. Jericho. I remember his name now. I try to control my anger, but I stand up and drop my napkin, the food settling in my stomach like a lead brick. I can't believe she did this to me.

"I don't understand," Noah says. "Is something wrong?"

"Let me ask you a question, Noah," I say, my voice flat.

I'm trying to control the urge to flee and the urge to punch him in the face. Here I thought I finally found a man I could like.

"Go." It's then I hear his voice. Mr. Sexy Voice. OMG, my luck can't be this bad. I've dreamed of this voice for weeks.

"How do you know Trina? And is Jericho with a department in Manhattan?" I step back from the table, putting distance between us.

"Yes, but how did you guess that?" he asks angrily. "And I don't know Trina. Jericho said you were a friend of a friend."

"I don't need a *pity* date. I already told Jericho he wasn't my type, but he had to have you, Mr. Sexy Voice, go out with me. I'm fucking done." I open my purse and throw some money on the table as his uncle makes his way over and they start talking.

I run for the door and step out onto the sidewalk to find it raining. Guess the weatherman was right. I don't have my jacket or umbrella. I just used my anytime cash and don't want to spend my emergency money, so I look for the nearest subway entrance and take off for it. Rain pelts down on me as I step out from under the awning. I'm less than half a block away from the restaurant, the rain is getting harder and feels like ice against my skin. My dress is soaked through and I finally decide I can't do this, I'm ruining my shoes. Fuck it. I step off the curb and hail a cab.

I slide in and pull the door closed behind me when it's yanked from my hand. Noah pushes me over and slides in next to me.

He rattles off an address a few blocks up further into the Upper East Side.

"I don't know what you're talking about, but this date is no pity date and you aren't getting away that easily." His arm wraps around me and pulls me close.

Old feelings of being controlled flash through my mind. I try to pull away, but he keeps me close. My body tightens in fear and I fight it down. I'm not that girl anymore. I'm a strong woman who can fight back now.

"I won't be told what to do and I won't be controlled," I tell him.

"Baby, the last thing I want to do is control you. I want a lot of things with you, but I won't control you. I want to know everything about you. I want you wild and testing me," he says, his voice dropping into a husky tone that makes me squeeze my legs together as he focuses on my lips.

I've never been drawn to a man this fast, not even the man who caused me to flee my family. His eyes rake my body and it feels like a caress against my chilled skin.

When we pull up outside a beautiful brownstone with classic lines, he pays the cabbie then steps out and reaches in for me. It's either now or never. His hand lingers in the air but he bends down to look at me. I look him in the eye and pray that in the last six years I've learned to see the evil before it's too late.

I slip my hand into his and he helps me out. He pushes me in front of him and wraps his arms wrap around my body. My skin is so chilled I lean into his warmth. He opens the gate and we walk up the stairs. He has to reach around me, wrapping those strong arms around me more to unlock the door. We step into the entry and again he pulls me in close to unlock the interior door. I step in and wait while he disengages the alarm system. I start to shiver again without his warmth surrounding me.

He takes one look at me and grabs my hand and leads me up the stairs.

"Oh no, mister. I might have come in here with you but we aren't sleeping together. I'm not that fucking easy." I pull my hand out of his and step back down onto the floor.

"I'm taking you up to my room so you can change. I'm sure one of my T-shirts is as long as that dress." He moves to grab my hand again as he steps back down. He's so tall and his arms so long he doesn't have to reach far.

"I said no." I step back toward the door, my right foot stepping back, prepared to fight him if I must.

His eyes watch my every move. "Okay, I'll go get you a

shirt to change into. I don't want my uncle's delivery guy to see everything under that dress when he brings our food in a moment."

"What?" I'm dumbfounded and relax slightly, shifting out of the defensive position. I stay by the door ready to flee if necessary.

He waves his hand and I look down. The sateen of the dress is plastered to my skin from my walk in the rain, and my darker pink bra can be faintly seen.

"Oh shit." I wrap my arms around my chest, trying to hide myself.

"Baby, I'll get you a shirt. You can change in the bathroom through the lounge." He points over my shoulder and I turn to see a small living room with shelves of books and brown leather furniture with fluffy cream pillows on it.

I step in and see this was the original library, but he has it set up as both a library and living room. All the shelves are full of books, some old leather-bound and some new. I walk around sliding my hand across all the exposed natural wood and books. In front of one of the windows is a large leather chair. I could curl up and read a book right there. The floors are hardwood with brown and cream-colored rugs.

"Here you go." His voice startles me and I jump, my hand going to my chest. He smiles as he hands me a large black T-shirt. He points through the other pocket door entrance to a hallway. "The bathroom is on the right."

I walk down the hallway and see the laundry area on one side and the bathroom on the other. I step in and take off my dress, then slip his shirt over my head and look down. My brothers would freak out if they saw me in the New Jersey Devils tee. I scrunch my hair now that it isn't straight anymore and check that my makeup doesn't look so bad. One thing living in Hawaii taught me was to wear waterproof makeup. I'm only wearing mascara, eyeliner, lipstick, and a little bronzer, nothing major.

I step out of the bathroom and grab a hanger for my dress, then hang it up on the rack over his washer and dryer between the cupboards. Hopefully it can dry somewhat before I leave.

I turn and follow the sounds of drawers opening and closing and find myself in the large kitchen. The room is not the original design, but it's beautiful. There is another doorway to the side and a walk-through to a large dining room with a fireplace. Noah is standing at a counter serving food onto plates. I walk over to him and help get us set up.

"My brothers would be pissed if they saw me in this T-shirt. They're die-hard Rangers fans."

He chuckles. "How many brothers do you have?"

Here we go again with the personal questions. I stop the instant panic and decide I do want to get to know him.

"I have two. They're both older than me."

"Nice. Do they live in the city?"

I don't know how to answer this question, so I try to come up with something. I honestly don't know where they live, only that they both work for FDNY. I wouldn't let Marco tell me what the family was up to because I didn't want to miss them more than I already did. I know that Marco left the military when I ran away.

"I honestly don't know. I moved away for several years and we haven't had contact since then." I tell him the truth. I'm shocked. "Wow, um, I've never shared that with anyone. It's awful to say but I don't know anything about my family anymore."

"It's not awful, but I bet it hurts. It sounds like you care for them a lot."

He takes both the plates and steps out into the dining room and pulls out a chair from the large round table. I don't sit down but walk to the wall of glass that overlooks the large back garden. I need the time to figure out how I can respond to his question.

"May I?" I ask as I point out the door.

"We can sit out there under the eaves if you want?"

"I'd like that."

He flips a switch then takes my hand to lead me out under the covered deck. When he releases my hand, I step out into the now drizzling rain to see the beautiful garden. I wish it was not raining. There are twinkle lights all over and a small bistro table with two chairs. There is a lounger that I would love to lay out and tan on. I can hear the trickle of water coming from the fountain at the back and I want to go check it out, but his voice stops me.

"Are you going to run through all my T-shirts playing in the rain?" He laughs and I join him at the table where he's placed our plates and a glass of wine for me. "Uncle Romeo sent your coat and even a bottle of Chianti for you."

"That's so sweet of him. Can you thank him for me?"

"I will. Can we try this again and explain why you think this is a pity date?"

"Okay." I sit down and take a bite of the lasagna again before I take a sip of the wine. After I swallow, I look at him. "My best friend works with me. I'm a 9-1-1 dispatcher for the city. She accidentally left her mic on when we were having a conversation about setting me up with a guy. Needless to say, every Manhattan fire department heard why I didn't want to date her friend. That evening your brother came by the center and asked me out. I told him he wasn't my type. I guess he and Trina decided to set us up. I'm sorry they played a trick on you like this."

"I'm not upset. I was having a good time and I know I still will once we get past this. What's the Mr. Sexy Voice comment about?"

God, I'd hoped he'd forgotten about that.

"I've dispatched you before." I bite my top lip trying to avoid saying anything else.

"So, you think my voice is sexy." He leans toward me and touches my chin to pull my lip from between my teeth.

"You know it is." I sigh.

"Why wouldn't you date the other guy?" His fingers brush my cheek and I find myself leaning into his hand.

"Um...because he was the same height as me," I mumble as I look down at my plate.

His fingers are back on my chin and lift it up so I'm looking at him.

"I'm glad because then you wouldn't be here with me. I love how tall you are." His voice is gruff, causing me to squeeze my legs together.

I want to crawl into his lap and kiss those lips and feel the scruff on his face against my hands. His hazel eyes drop to my lips and I like them.

He groans. "Eat, baby, before I say fuck it and kiss the shit out of you."

"Okay." I hear the tremble in my voice.

We enjoy our meal and make small talk, nothing major again. He shares more than I do. As usual I don't offer specifics about my life, just generals. I catch him watching me several times.

"How long have you been back in the city?"

"I moved back in November."

"Jer said you lived out west."

"Yeah." I don't offer any more information.

"You are harder to break than some of the perps I inter-rogate." He laughs, and I smile.

"Okay, I've only been back in the city for six months, before that I lived in Hawaii for five and a half years."

"Wow. Why there?"

"I'd always wanted to go and it was the farthest away I could get without needing a passport or freezing."

"Did you like it?"

"Yeah, I loved it. The million people on a tiny island wasn't my favorite, but it's like the island of Manhattan. I loved the jungles and plants. I loved my job and friends."

"Not that I'm not glad you came back, but why did you if you liked it so much?"

"My father had a heart attack. I wanted to be close if the family needed me."

"How's he doing now?"

"He's getting better but he was forced to retire from his job with the transit authority. "

"So, you've been able to see him?"

I know he's questioning me because I told him earlier I didn't see my family. I don't know why I feel the need to be honest with him.

"Actually, I saw him once, but we didn't get to talk and I had to leave right away. It was so hard to have them that close and not hug them."

"That's gotta be hard. I'm surprised your mama didn't come after you, mine would have."

"Oh, she tried, but I was faster. It's for the best. Well, I should probably be going." I look at my wrist and see it's almost eleven. I can't tell him it's to protect them that I stay away. That if I try, they'll all be hurt. I keep those secrets to myself.

"I'll drive you."

"No, I can take a cab."

"Afraid of me knowing where you live?" He jokes and the urge to say yes is strong. I don't like anyone knowing too much about me.

"Come on," he says as he stands and turns back to the house.

I take in the long lines of muscle across his back as they flex under his shirt while he moves in front of me. I help him clean up then go to retrieve my dress and change back into it. It's still damp but it'll do until I get home.

I step out and he takes me in. "I left your T-shirt on the washer for you."

"You could've kept it." He offers.

"I'm okay."

He walks me out the back, holding my umbrella as he leads me through the yard and into a garage where a black Jeep Rubicon is parked. He opens the door and helps me in. He doesn't close the door until he sees me buckle up.

We make our way across Manhattan toward the Bronx. When we pull up to my building and I go to get out, he stops me. He turns off the jeep and gets out and walks around to my side. We walk to the building entrance with our hands clasped together. His large hand and strong fingers are laced with mine and I take in his tanned skin against my pale skin under the street lights. He stops at the door and turns to face me.

"I'm not going to push to walk you inside because I can sense how much this is bothering you. But, Kenzie, baby, I want to see you again. Can I have your number?"

I nod, dumbfounded by his admission. I want to see more of him and I'm glad he isn't pushing me tonight. He hands me his phone and I type my number into it. He immediately texts me so I have his number. He leans in and I catch my breath waiting for those lips to touch mine, but they don't.

"Good night, beautiful." He kisses my forehead. His breath wafting over my skin.

"Night, Mr. Sexy Voice." I sigh and disengage my hand from his. He doesn't want to let me go and I don't want him to. Something about him feels right.

I turn to the door and open it up. Once I'm through, I turn back and wave at him. He waves and heads back to his vehicle. I watch him walk away and shake myself to head up to my apartment.

As I approach my door, my good mood slips away. A glint of gold catches my eye. Hanging from my door handle is a necklace I haven't seen in years. I whip around looking for him, expecting him to come barreling out of the shadows, but I see nothing.

I leave the necklace there and immediately take off back down the hall. I pull up the Uber app and schedule a ride. I'm running back out into the night as it's pulling up. I jump in and confirm I want to go to Times Square. It's the busiest place and I know I'll be able to lose him in the crowds, even at this time of night. The hair on the back of my neck stands up and I know he's out here watching me.

Oh God, he saw Noah.

The driver drops me off and I walk into the first hotel. I put my hair up, slip my raincoat off and drop it along with the umbrella in a seat, then I walk right back out with the first group that walks by. I mix in as if I'm with them. I break off into another hotel and walk to the counter to book a room, using the emergency cash I have hidden in a pocket of my wallet. As soon as I get into my room, I close the blinds and sit down trying to plan out my next steps. Maybe

I need to trust someone finally. I text the number for my room and wait to shut off my cell phone.

How did he find me? Where did I mess up? I know he didn't follow me from work, but how else could he have found me? Somehow, I'll have to take care of him.

CHAPTER FIVE

NOAH

Last night was one of the most enjoyable nights I've had in a long time. I hate that I have to work on Saturday, or I'd call her and try to get a second date with her.

"What's the grin for, Caine?" Linc asks.

"Just thinking about last night."

"Yeah? Well wipe the grin off your face, we have a family to question."

"Did the original detectives get back to you?" I called them but I left both mine and Linc's contact information.

"Yep. Winthrop was dating a girl that disappeared only days before he did. One Kenzie Graco. She hasn't returned as far as background checks confirm, but she was only a teenager at the time with a clean record, so no prints or reports in the system. Family finally pulled the missing person's report several months ago. Makes you wonder if she came back or if they found her."

It's a rare name but the last name is different, so I don't

say anything. My duty wants me to tell my partner about the possible coincidence, but my honor to her is already stronger and I'll protect her.

When we get to the house in Bensonhurst, only a few down from the grandmother's, I look at the driveway full of vehicles. Two have firefighter association stickers. We walk up to the door and Linc knocks. A man a little shorter than me answers the door. His dark hair is long and hangs over his forehead, but his eyes look familiar to me. They are gray and instantly my gut clenches. Fuck no!

"Yeah." His accent is thick, and he stands blocking our view from most of the home behind him.

"We are looking for the Graco family." Linc supplies.

We both produce our shields and a woman walking behind him sees us and immediately drops what she's carrying. She starts chanting no over and over.

Another dark-haired guy, his hair shorter, walks up and takes her in his arms as an older man comes to the door. He's bigger than the man who answered the door, but he carries himself as if he's weak or sick.

"Is this about our daughter?" His voice is torn up and I can feel the pain radiating off him.

"Hello, sir. I'm Detective Warren and this is my partner Detective Caine. We would like to speak to Kenzie Graco, if we could?"

"She's not here." He doesn't say anything else.

"We'd like to talk to her about Thomas Winthrop."

"He was my daughter's high school sweetheart. He went missing just days after she did."

"She's still missing?"

He shakes his head no.

"Do you know where she is? We'd like to ask her a few questions."

44

"Keni has only been here once, six months ago, we haven't seen her since." The man supplies. Something about his story sounds similar to another story I've heard recently.

"We are investigating the death of Mr. Winthrop, and his grandmother. We need to rule out your daughter." Linc pushes while I observe the family.

The older man steps back, allowing us entrance.

"I know how to reach her." The long-haired son offers as we step into the house.

"What do mean?" The older man turns to look at him.

"It's why she came home. After your heart attack, I found a way to find her. Then a couple weeks ago she texted me. I have her number."

All the information causes my gut to clench tighter. It sounds eerily familiar. I look around the room again. The woman and what must be the older son walked into the kitchen.

"I'm Salvatore and this is my son Marco. My other son Lorenzo and my wife, Francesca, are in the other room. It's been my wife's worst fear that one day the police will come tell us our daughter is dead."

"Your daughter, Kenzie, do you know where she works or anything?" Linc asks.

"No, I don't know about her new life. Kenzie couldn't stay because Roy saw her when she tried to visit with us."

Can it be the same? I trust my gut, it's never steered me wrong before.

"Kenzie's last name same as yours?" I ask.

"Yes. Graco," he states.

"Do you have a picture of her?" My gut won't stop and until I see her, I won't rule it out.

He stands and walks to the mantle behind him and picks up a picture. He hands it to me.

45

It could be a coincidence. Can't it?

Except the picture is of a young Kenzie. My Kenzie. Her blond hair is in braids down each side of her head, her smile so bright my chest pulls. She's in a school uniform. She smiled last night but nothing like this. I want to see this smile.

Her mother walks back in and points out another picture on the wall. It's of the victim and Kenzie dressed for what appears to be prom. This young Kenzie doesn't have the shadows of sorrow and pain like the woman I know. Her mom points to one more picture where Kenzie is more subdued. No smile. She's in a cap and gown for graduation. The man holding her protectively is about her height, older for sure, and has a grip on her that even in the picture shows control.

"Who's the man?" I ask, sure I know the answer.

"That's Roy Tramble. The man that stole my baby," her mom says in a voice tight with pain. Her face is pinched, and tears slowly roll down her face.

I look at her, one eyebrow dropping as the other raises in a silent question.

"He convinced her we were controlling her and holding her back. Then he made her choose us or him. When she said us, he threatened to kill himself. My Kenzie has such a soft heart she didn't want him to hurt himself, so she chose him in the end. Two months later my baby was gone. He was still here, so I think she ran from him too. I don't know why she just didn't come home to us. We're her family." She begs me to answer questions I can't without giving away that I know her.

Linc steps up to us as we are talking.

"The brother hasn't gotten a response. Her messages aren't being read. She must have her phone off."

"Is there any reason she would hurt Thomas?" I ask the group.

"No, she wouldn't, but Roy would. Besides, I saw Tommy after Keni ran. He and Roy were arguing," Lorenzo says.

"When was that?" Linc asks.

"A few days after Keni ran away. I was out looking for her and saw them. They were outside a local hangout that Tommy and Keni would visit."

"Thank you for your help." I give them my card. "If you hear from her or remember anything else, please call us."

"Detective Caine, when she tried to come see us six months ago, Ms. Winthrop saw Roy and was yelling at him to leave. We have a lifetime restraining order against him," Mr. Graco says.

"We'll look into him for you." I offer.

When we get out to the car, I look at Linc.

"I know where she is. She's going by Russo and I had dinner with her last night. She didn't kill our victim, but I wouldn't be surprised if this Roy asshole did."

"Address," is all he says, and we make our way to her apartment. When we arrive the landlord tells us Kenzie up and moved out this morning. He shows us to her studio apartment and we find a necklace hanging from the door handle. We bag it as evidence before stepping inside. The apartment was furnished but there are plants everywhere. She wouldn't have left them unless she had to. My girl was so entranced with my garden, I know she loves plants. So, I do what I can for her.

"We'll take all the plants."

Linc looks at me like I've lost my mind.

"When did she leave?" I ask the landlord.

"She came by a couple hours ago with a friend of hers and her husband."

"Do you know this friend's name?"

"No, but I've seen her here a couple times in the last few months. I believe they work together."

"Thank you for your cooperation. Here is my card, call me if you see or hear from her."

"Is she in trouble? She's such a nice, quiet girl."

"We just need to ask her some questions."

He's right, she is quiet and one of the sweetest women I know. I need to find her because I'm certain this Roy asshole is after her too.

We head out as I look at the necklace in the bag. It's a rose gold crown surrounded by a titanium band that says, "Keep Me in Your Heart." It's not the Kenzie I met last night's style, but maybe it was before. A thought hits me and I turn back around to look at the landlord.

"Sir, when did this necklace show up? Was it here after she left?"

"No, it was here before she left. I asked her several times if she wanted to take it and she said she didn't want it. I do remember her friend making a comment about it and Kenzie said it was there last night. I'm surprised no one stole it, but that shows you her effect on people. All the neighbors like her."

"You heard her say it was here last night?" An awful feeling churns in my gut.

"Yeah."

"Do you know if she came home last night?" I know I dropped her off here but she could have turned around and walked out.

"Her friend said something about a hotel."

"Thank you."

As I walk out to put the first load of plants in the car, the hair on the back of my neck stands up. Not being obvious, I check out my surroundings. I see a car with a guy sitting in it a few cars down but I don't let on that I see him. As I pass Linc going back for another load I let him know.

"We're being watched. Fifth car behind ours. See if you can get the plate."

"On it."

We finish packing the car with her plants and head to my place to drop them off. Neither of us were able to get the plate as there was no front plate on the car. We lose the car on our way to the Upper East Side.

"You're fucking a witness, Noah. You need to give me all the information you have and step back." Linc rages at me as I unlock the door to my brownstone.

The urge to pound him into the pavement is so great, I grind my teeth and tighten my jaw. Normally I'm questioning Linc and his loose ways but here he is questioning me.

"I know as much as you do, except I do know where she works. I'm not fucking her, and if you ever talk about her like that again, I'll be finding a new partner after I break your jaw." I step up into his face and look down on him.

"Whoa, buddy. You're that serious about her?"

"Yes." My response is immediate and full of the conviction in my heart. I know she didn't hurt anyone.

"Okay, where does she work?"

"For us, she's a dispatcher."

After I settle her plants around the dining room, I text her again trying to get her to respond to me.

"I called the dispatch center, she's off until Monday. Let's head back to the precinct and see what we can find out about this Roy character."

We head out and all weekend I don't hear from her, and the more we learn about Roy Tramble bothers me. I send the necklace to forensics to see if they can get anything from it.

MONDAY MORNING I'm sitting at my desk frustrated because we found out Kenzie has called out sick for the next couple of days. There are two more people I want to question about her whereabouts. I sent Jer a text earlier to meet me for lunch, and as I walk up to the small pizzeria he chose, I pray he can direct me to her. I know in my gut she's in danger and that's why she ran.

"Hey, bro, what's up? Your text was cryptic," Jericho asks as I take a seat across from him in the booth.

He's in his usual style of cargo EMT pants and a station T-shirt. Jer is just an inch shorter than me and trim. His hair is dark brown like mine. But while Zeke and I take after our father with his hazel eyes, Jer has the blue eyes of our mother.

"I need to ask you about Kenzie."

"Thought you had a date with her Friday night." He takes a big bite of his folded pizza slice.

"Yeah, but she disappeared Saturday."

He starts laughing. "You scared her away." He chokes on his food and takes a sip of his soda to swallow it down.

"No. She's actually a part of a case I'm investigating, and I need to get to her before she gets hurt."

"Dude, really?" His eyebrows draw up.

"Yep."

"She works for dispatch. Her friend is named Trina

Acosta. I have her number, just a sec." He wipes his hands off after putting his pizza down and pulls out his phone.

"I know she works for dispatch. By the way, she thought she was a pity date. Dude, she is so not that."

"So, you like her?" He smiles.

"Hell yeah. She's mine."

"Really?" He cocks his head to the side.

"Fuck yeah."

"Okay, here you go. I texted you her info. From what I understand, Kenzie works Monday through Thursday but rotates days and nights weekly."

"Yeah, that's what I got when I called dispatch. She's on days right now, but she called out today."

"Can you tell me what's going on?"

"Yeah, 'cause Kenzie is coming home with me if she's in a hotel. She has an ex-boyfriend who is a lot whacked. I'm not sure if he threatened her, but he is the lead suspect in a cold case I'm working."

"Fuck, man. I'll keep an eye out for her too."

"Thanks."

We eat and talk about plans for the rest of the week. Jer's schedule with FDNY rotates around from night and day shifts, so he comes and goes quite a bit. He's quiet most of the time, so I don't mind him living with me.

"I need to get back to the station. I guess Zeke will be here on Wednesday?"

"Yeah, he'll stay at our place instead of Mom's 'cause he has meetings with the FBI and NYPD regarding a case he's working."

"Cool. I'm out."

We both stand and he thumps me on the back as he takes off. The station he works at is around the block from here. I head back to the precinct so I can call Kenzie's friend Trina.

Trina's phone goes to voicemail and I leave a detailed message asking her to call me back. I don't ask about Kenzie and I don't let on that it has anything to do with her. Just that I need to speak to Trina about an ongoing case.

CHAPTER SIX

KENZIE

I look at the clock in the corner of one of the monitors. Another twenty minutes until my shift is done and I'm out of here.

"Russo, my office," my supervisor says from his office door.

I signal I heard him and finish the call I'm working on, then I sign out as busy and stand from my chair. As I turn to look in his office, I see Noah's large back and dark hair. He's in black slacks and jacket. I'd recognize him in a crowd. Fuck. Against my will, my body tingles wanting him.

What is he doing here? I know he called Trina with some lie about an ongoing case. I guess my silent treatment didn't give him the hint. But I need him to leave me alone so Roy doesn't focus on him next.

I've left my phone off this whole time in fear Roy can trace me. I still don't know how he found me. I didn't want to ask Trina for help but she's all I have, and it's time to trust someone. Besides, Roy wouldn't go after her because her husband wouldn't think twice about going after him.

Trina's husband works Customs and Border Patrol, he bench presses small cars. He went with us and together we got me settled into another hotel in Manhattan. They wanted me to come stay with them in Queens, but they've already done too much. I didn't want to put them in any more harm than necessary.

I look at the clock again trying to figure out if I can sneak out and handle my supervisor tomorrow. I look toward the door and see another man with blondish hair standing there with his arms crossed over his chest. He's watching me like he knows I want to flee.

Okay, time to pull up my big girl panties.

"Hello," I say as I stand in the entrance to my supervisor's office.

Noah turns and I take in the burgundy tie with his white shirt. The shirt pulls across his pecs and the jacket is fitted across his arms. His clothes must be custom made to his size.

"This way." Noah leads us to the conference room and motions for me to walk in first. He follows me in with the blond guy behind him and closes the door. He must be Noah's partner. How did Noah get him involved?

"Look, it was one date. A nice date, but I'm not interested in anything more." I start.

"Sit, Ms. Russo, or should I say, Ms. Graco?" Noah's voice has a bite to it and I whip my head around to look at him.

His brows are dropped, his lips pinched. I haven't been called Graco in years. It takes me a second to realize he's mad at me for lying, and I gather this has to do with something more than me not returning a phone call.

"My legal name is Russo." I settle that question. I wasn't lying.

"When did you have it changed?"

"A while ago."

"How long?"

"It doesn't matter."

He teased me before about being worse than a perp. He's going to find out just how worse if he doesn't change his attitude soon.

"Your family doesn't know?"

"My family has nothing to do with us." I wave my hand between us.

"You see, babe, that's where you're wrong. Everything about you has to do with *us*." He waves his hand just like I did. "But I'm not talking about us yet. How do you know Thomas Winthrop?"

"He's a friend." I swallow, trying to figure out what Tommy has to do with this. I remember the call from a couple weeks ago at Tommy's old address and pray that wasn't about him.

"Ms. Russo, I'm Detective Warren and you know Detective Caine, we are from the cold case division."

I nod because I already knew that. Noah delved into what kind of work he did over dinner on Friday.

"When was the last time you saw Mr. Winthrop?"

I pause and pull my lips between my teeth. Do I answer honestly? That choice is taken from me when Noah interrupts my thoughts.

"Kenzie, we need to know exactly when you saw him last. We already have a time line, so we'll know if you're lying. I know you moved away six years ago."

I look him in the eye. "I haven't seen Tommy since before I left." I bite my lips, I want to know. I need to know. "Did you talk to my family?" The question comes out no matter how much I try not to let it.

"Yes. They're worried about you." Noah reaches across the table and takes my hand. I flip my hand over so our palms are against each other's. The tingles from before are still there.

"Tommy..." I look down at the table and try to push the tears back. "He helped me." I swallow again. "He hired an attorney to meet me in Detroit to change my name. He helped me get the money together so I could go to Hawaii." I look up, feeling the burn in my nose, the tears on the edge of my lids.

"Fuck, baby," Noah exclaims as he pushes back and rounds the table. He pulls me up and into his arms. "We found his body a couple of weeks ago. He's dead."

"Oh God." I start but my breathing gets out of control. No, not Tommy.

I can't hold back the tears as Noah holds me tighter and whispers calming words in my ear. I pull away and push him back. He needs to know this.

"I didn't kill him. I swear, but..." I choke on the words and hold my hand up so Noah can't come to me again. "It's my fault. He's dead because of me."

"I'm sorry, Ms. Russo, but we're going to have to take you in for questioning," Detective Warren says and I jolt from the pain. I'm going to lose everything because of Roy.

"No, we don't. You heard her say she didn't kill him," Noah says with a growl in his voice as he faces off with his partner.

"No, it's okay, Noah. I understand." I try to calm him. I don't want him to get in trouble for helping me.

I know I should keep him at arm's length so Roy doesn't come after him too. Roy saw us together the other night, I know he did. And I can't allow Noah to jeopardize his career for me.

I look between the two of them and try to come up with a plan. I've got an idea but it means I'll have to run permanently.

"Let me clock out and get my bag and I'll go with you." I offer and Noah watches me. He tries to reach for me again but I step back further and walk around the table toward the door.

I stop and turn to look at Noah. This will be the last time I get to look at him. His big body is tense and his jaw is clenched. I bite my top lip, holding it between my teeth, wanting to take him all in. The memories will be all that I have. I pull my shoulders back and stand taller. For the second time in my life, I'm leaving those I care about to protect them.

I turn away and walk to the locker room where I swipe my badge to clock out and take my bag from my locker. I write a quick note to Trina telling her goodbye and explaining why I need to leave. I know I don't have much more time, so I slip my bag over my shoulder and head out the side door that leads directly to the stairwell. I make it to the bottom of the stairs and open the exit door when I hear Noah yell "fuck."

I give the cabbie the address to a hotel near where I'm staying so they don't have my exact location. Leaning my head back, I take in everything that has transpired and my heart clenches. How can I care about Noah so quickly? I just met him.

NOAH

When she stops at the door and turns to look at me, I see devastation in her eyes. The gray so dark it's stormy looking from across the room. I want to go to her, but I know I shouldn't. She's a suspect. But in my gut, I know she didn't do it. I watch as her shoulders go back and her spine straightens. She's so strong.

We wait for a few more minutes and that's when I realize what she was doing. She was saying goodbye to me.

"Fuckin A." I grit out as I take off out the room and head for the locker room. "Coming in," I yell as I enter the empty locker room. I see another exit and run over. "Fuck," I yell when I throw it open and hear the door at the bottom of the stairs open too. I turn and look at Linc. "She just gave us the slip."

"I'm going to have to put out a BOLO on her," he says, then radios the information for all units to be on the lookout.

"Fuck, I know."

"You're going to want to tell the captain you're involved with a suspect."

"Obviously she doesn't consider us an item, so, no, I'm not going to tell him yet." I growl as we walk out.

We inform her supervisor to contact us immediately if she contacts the dispatch office or shows up. The BOLO won't allow her to fly out of New York, but if she drives out far enough to get to another airport, she can get away, unless she's spotted.

"I'll drop you at your place and then I'll go fill out paper-work, seeing as your brother is in town." Linc offers.

"Nope, I'll go with you."

"What if we head over to Queens and question her friend? She knows where Kenzie is staying."

"Let's do it."

I watch out the window as we work our way through the city traffic to Queens. When we get to Trina's place, she won't give us any information and lawyers up.

"Look, if you hear from her, please tell her to call us. We just need to ask her some questions," I implore her.

"Listen here, fuck face, she's my best friend. I won't tell you anything. Also, she won't tell me what's going on with her. I was shocked she even asked me for help on Saturday," she says.

"Why?" Linc asks.

"That's all I'm saying. You can leave or haul me in," she says and her husband steps up behind her.

"Guys, you're out now," he says as he folds his large arms over his chest. He's not as tall as me but he's wider with more muscle.

CHAPTER SEVEN

KENZIE

I can't stay here at the hotel. I know a BOLO is out on me by now as it's standard procedure. And I won't be able to fly either. I pace around my hotel room and decide I can't take this anymore. I grab my gym bag and a change of clothes and head out to the gym I like to work out at.

I've not only studied Brazilian jiu-jitsu but also kickboxing. I don't feel like joining a class or working out with someone else, so I change and head for a practice dummy.

I slip my ear buds in and blare my music while I start with stretches then proceed to beat up the dummy. Every hit is a hit I wish I could inflict on Roy. I've allowed him to destroy so much of my life. Manipulating me, hit to the gut. Making me choose, kick to the face. Hurting me, shin kick to the leg. Punches, kicks, blocks come through my body and I attack the dummy. I attack the dummy like I want to attack Roy.

After years of therapy I learned it wasn't just my fault. He used me. Hurt me. He lied to me. Each hit to the dummy is like a balm to my soul, squeezing the festering wound that used to be my heart. A heart I kept locked up until Noah. I see his face float into my vision, and I fall to the mats. Tears roll down my face, and I'm thankful I'm in a room by myself so no one can see me.

As I kneel there, I realize how tired I am. Tired of running. Tired of hiding. Tired of not letting someone in. I stand up and look at the dummy, my shoulders ache but I pull them back. I know how to protect myself now. I can fight and I'm licensed to conceal and carry. I'm done running. I can't do this anymore and I know who I can ask for help. Right now.

I shower in the locker room and wish I could go back to the hotel and soak in the tub, but I need to take care of this now. I slip into a pair of skinny blue jeans, a blue round neck T-shirt, a tan jacket, and my brown ankle booties. I swipe on some mascara and lip gloss after I pile all my hair up on top of my head into a messy bun. Well, at least I'll look good for my mug shots if I'm arrested. I lock down that thought because I didn't do anything wrong.

I walk out of the gym carrying my bag and give the cabbie the cross street for Noah's brownstone. I don't know the exact address, but I'll know it when I see it. I pull my bag in tight to my body, the heaviness of it soothes me.

When the cabbie drops me off at the corner, I look around and realize I'm on the wrong side of the street. I cross over and go about a third of the way down the block before I stop. I recognize the gate, door, and planters. It's ten o'clock at night, but I see lights on and figure he's still awake. Looking at the street, I see the unmarked squad car parked at the curb. He either brought it home or his partner is here. I take in his house, the large windows, the planters that make me wonder when he has time to work on them. I need to go knock before one of his neighbors looks out and sees me standing here. I don't want the police called.

Okay, big girl panties.

I open the gate and close it behind me before I start up the stairs to the main level. I can see lights on in the basement windows and what looks like movement. I ring the bell and wait. I look around me again, my nerves getting the best of me. I don't feel like someone is watching me, but I don't feel comfortable either. I'm at a loss right now as to what I actually feel. I want Noah to want me, but after he knows what I did, will he still feel the same?

I ring the bell again and look over the edge of the stone railing to see more movement downstairs. A light flips on in the vestibule between the doors, then the light over my head goes on. I jump back down a step and shield my eyes from the brightness. A large man opens the door. He's not as tall or as broad as Noah but his eyes are the same. His dark hair is slightly longer and he has a beard.

"Yeah?" he asks and I continue to stand there.

I don't know what to say. I don't know what I *should* say.

"Are you going to say something or just stand there, girly?" His voice is gruffer and he's angry. "Look, I'm missing the—"

He's pushed to the side and an angry Noah is standing over me blocking the light. I can't see his eyes in the darkness, but his brows are dropped and his jaw is locked and tight.

"I-I'm. So s-s-sorry." Tears spring to my eyes.

"Baby!" He lifts me in his arms, and I bury my face in his neck, taking in his spicy musk and leather scent.

He turns and carries me into the house, past his brothers and partner. My legs are dangling against his, so he hikes me up his body and I wrap my legs around him. One of his hands goes to my ass, the other against my back. I bury my face further into his neck and kiss the side of it, taking in his smell and letting it calm me. He sits down on the chaise lounge in the garden with me straddling him. I start to move off him and he holds me tighter. He's still in his clothes from earlier. The jacket is gone and the sleeves are rolled up showing his impressive forearms.

"I don't want to run anymore," I say, looking him in the eye. The green has overtaken the brown, leaving only a ring of the dark color visible.

"I'll protect you," he swears as he pulls my lips to his, and I finally have his lips where I've wanted them. They are firm and full. His tongue touches my lips and I open as he angles my head to go deeper, claiming my mouth. Claiming me.

Every thought escapes my mind and I allow him to take the kiss deeper as he pulls me in closer. I feel his erection at my core and rock against it. He groans and pulls away.

"Please don't ever walk around at night again."

"I know how to fight, and I have my gun," I say as I straighten.

He's questioning if I can take care of myself. I feel the anger like a spark to my desire and I purse my lips in frustration.

"Your what?" His head swings back, and I realize I just admitted to a cop I have a gun. Oh well, get over it, bucko.

"I have a permit to carry it." I defend myself.

"Fuck, baby," he growls as he grabs my neck and pulls me back down to his lips.

Another searing kiss and I could care less what I need to tell him until a throat clears from behind us.

"Sorry to interrupt, but I canceled the BOLO," his partner says and my body stiffens.

"Just a moment, Linc." Noah grits out. "Okay, baby, we

need you to answer some questions. Are you ready?"

"Yes." I start but he puts his finger to my lips.

"First, you better message Trina and tell her you're safe. We went to question her about your whereabouts. She told us she would lawyer up and plead the fifth before she gave you up."

"Oh my God. That woman is crazy." I laugh as I disentangle myself from Noah. "But I can't use my phone, well, at least I don't think I can."

"Use mine." He hands me his and I send her a quick text.

She responds letting me know if I need her she'll come get me. I thank her and tell her I love her, then I hand the phone back to Noah. She is one of the reasons I'm here. I don't want her to get in trouble now that she's just found out she is expecting after years of trying. I can't let her get hurt because of my fucked-up past, but I don't want to lose any more friends or family than I already have.

Noah takes my hand and leads me into the house. We've barely crossed over the threshold when my stomach lets out a loud rumble.

"When was the last time you ate, baby," Noah asks as he turns to me.

I bite the side of my lip trying to remember. "Lunch?" I question, not even sure I ate then.

"Sit. I'll get you something. We can talk here."

I sit down as the other three men sit around the table. The man that answered the door sits on my right, next to him and across from me is Noah's partner, and finally Jericho is sitting next to the empty chair to my left. Noah returns and sets a chicken Caesar salad down in front of me with a glass of white wine. I take a large swallow, needing some liquid courage for what I'm about to confess, and immediately feel it hit my empty stomach. I need to put some food in me, but I sit back and wait for them to question me instead.

"Eat, baby, at least a couple bites, then we'll talk."

I feel uncomfortable and on display as I sit there for a moment.

Finally, the man on my right reaches out but doesn't touch me. I still flinch back, the memories are too close not to. Immediately Noah growls and his arm lands on the back of my chair.

"I'm Zeke, by the way. I'm not going to hurt you, but as the only person here not a part of NYPD or FDNY, I'm on your side. Do you need to contact an attorney? Because I know several," he says as he looks at me. His lips tip up at the corner and I calm slightly.

"No. I didn't do anything wrong. It took years for me to understand that, but I didn't break any laws. However, I know Tommy was hurt because of me."

"Fucking perfect. Zeke, whose side are you on offering her an attorney?" Noah's partner says.

Noah's arm flexes around me but Zeke jumps in before Noah can say anything.

"Looking at the way my brother is acting, I have a feeling dollface here will be permanent. I've always wanted a little sister, even tried to talk Ma into taking Jer back and getting me one. Now I have one and I'm going to be on her side. So, fuck police procedure right now. Family comes first," he growls out as he slides his chair away from Linc. Jericho moves closer to Noah, and we are all on one side of the table.

"Wait, um." They can't do this for me. "You don't know what I'm going to tell you. I've done some awful, mean things. I'm not your family and you don't want me to be. I threw away my own family. Besides, Noah isn't going—"

Noah stands and pulls my chair back, then picks me up and deposits me on his lap. He turns my face to his.

"Baby, you're mine. I know what happened with your family and you didn't throw them away. I'm fairly certain you're protecting them, aren't you?"

Do I tell him the truth? Roy will kill everyone if I tell on him. I pull my top lip between my teeth, the nervous habit coming out strong. Slightly so it's almost imperceptible, I nod my head and look down.

"Fuck," all of them exclaim, including Linc.

"Please eat," Noah says as he turns me back to the table but doesn't release me.

I take a bite of the chicken and romaine. Then pop a crouton into my mouth after I swallow my first bite. I take another bite and realize I'm famished but the food still feels like a lead brick. I need to tell them the truth. I push the plate away again and look at them. Before I can tell them my story, I need to ask another important question.

"Why are you investigating Tommy's murder if you're cold case detectives?" I ask Linc.

"Why don't you tell us why you think you're responsible and then I'll tell you?"

"Because Roy found out Tommy helped me. That's the only way. But it's been six years and Roy hasn't hurt him until now. You said you found his body two weeks ago. When was he killed?" I do the math in my head, I only had one more payment to make.

"Baby, Tommy's been dead for six years," Noah says.

My hands clench and my body starts trembling. My breathing becomes erratic like I can't catch my breath. This has happened before. I start fighting Noah trying to get away. It can't be true. It can't be. I shake my head back and forth. Someone chants no over and over. It's not until two strong hands cup my cheeks and a voice breaks through the fog that I realize it's me.

"Dollface! Look at me. Open your eyes," Zeke commands.

Slowly I open my eyes. I feel strong arms wrapped around me, but I focus on the eyes. Hazel eyes so similar to Noah's, a grittier voice than his but a tone that soothes me right now.

"We got you. Deep breath in through your nose, hold it, exhale slowly."

I do as he says, and my head stops swimming. How does he know that's what I need?

"Keep looking at me. Focus on me."

I relax my hands realizing they are clenched so tight my fingers ache. Noah places soft kisses against my back and the back of my neck. Zeke's thumbs caress my cheeks. I close my eyes slowly and open them again to look at him.

"Focus on me only, dollface, and tell me what you need to," he commands again in a gruff voice.

"How can Tommy be dead for six years? I've been paying him every month." My voice quivers as I ask the question I desperately need the answer to.

"What do you mean, baby?" Noah's voice rumbles through my body.

"He gave me money to pay for my name change, to get me to Hawaii, and to help me get set up. Without him I wouldn't be here right now."

The shaking starts up again. I feel like my body is chilled.

"Focus on me, dollface, I don't want you to faint. Let's take another deep breath." Again, he directs me to take a cleansing breath and I do. "Okay, start from the beginning. How long have you known Tommy?"

It's an easy question.

"I've known...oh, wait. I knew him since we were in grade school. He went to public schools, but I was always in private schools. In high school we dated for a few years but our senior year he wanted to try seeing other girls at his school. So, we broke up. I was just a volleyball playing book-worm. I didn't socialize much. A friend invited me to a party at her house and I met this older guy. I didn't realize he was ten years older than me. I just listened to his stories. He had traveled all over. He told me he was a crab fisherman and ice road trucker in Alaska, and he said he was a bodyguard for a movie star in L.A. He said he couldn't tell me which star. I never questioned the stories, I thought they were real. The furthest I'd ever traveled to was Coney Island. Papa was always working. Before Roy told me all of the places and things he'd done, I lived vicariously through my brother Marco who was in the Army. I was lost to everything that was him. I did what he said." I pause, aware of what comes next, but don't know if I can say it out loud.

"You're safe, dollface, keep going," Zeke says and I look at him again. His hands still holding my face.

"When he found out I wasn't a virgin, he got mad at me and stopped talking to me for days." The groan of pain and tightening of his arms lets me know Noah is upset. "I was devastated. I called him over and over, but he would send my calls to voice mail. Finally, he came to see me after school one day. My parents were upset and told him to leave me alone. They called the police, but because I was so close to eighteen the police wouldn't do anything. He took me into New York and said that for us to continue seeing each other I had to give him everything. I didn't know what he meant. He said I needed to give up my family and be with him. I told him I couldn't do that. He opened the door to his car and pushed me out onto the sidewalk." Another growl, this time not just from Noah but I think Jericho. "I didn't know where I was, but I got to a transit officer and had them call my papa."

Tears slide down my face and hiccups erupt from my body. The pain of that day is still so raw and real. Zeke brushes away the tears.

"Papa took me home. I was grounded and told I couldn't see Roy anymore. I told them I wouldn't choose him over my family." God what a lie. "I confessed he didn't use a condom and my mama cried. The next day they took me to the clinic and had me tested. I wasn't pregnant so they started me on the shot. My parents were upset but they didn't want Roy to have any more control over me than he already did."

Here comes the hardest part. I look down to avoid Zeke's eyes. "I thought my life would return to normal. Volleyball practice started and I was focused on the last semester of my senior year. I still didn't know what I wanted to do after school, but I didn't care. In February Roy showed up outside the school. It had been over a month since I'd seen him last. He begged for my forgiveness, but I couldn't do it. I was still so hurt and raw. I wouldn't leave my family, they loved me. I went home that night and was in my room studying when my cell went off. I know now it was another form of manipulation, but I was so young and naive." A gentle kiss against the side of my neck has me turning to look back at Noah. He's going to hate me now. I close my eyes and try to avoid him. Avoid the truth. Avoid the pain.

"Kenzie, look at me, dollface." Zeke's voice breaks through the returning panic.

I open my eyes and continue.

"He said if he couldn't live with me, he'd rather be dead. I ran. I ran out the door and wasn't sure where I was going until lights flipped on and I saw his car. I jumped in and begged him not to do it. I told him I loved him, and he was my family. We hid our relationship for a week, then on Valentine's Day he got me a necklace with a crown. Said I was his queen. He always called me his queen and he was my king.

"My parents eventually found out and confronted us, and I moved out, but they made me promise I would keep going to school. Roy didn't have a place to live, so we stayed on the sofa of a friend of his. Sometimes we stayed in his car, and even at a hostel once. I thought it was an adventure. He would get mad at me for going to school. He said it was another form of control by my parents. But I promised and I don't go back on my promises. Then at the end of March he found out I was on birth control and beat me. I had bruises everywhere and couldn't even raise one of my arms over my head. My ribs were bruised so bad I couldn't breathe. I wanted to leave. God did I ever, but he threatened to kill my papa and Enzo."

I drop my eyes again and take a deep breath before I can continue. I let my life become so messed up. I let my family become targets for a mad man.

"He was working for one of the *families* at the time. He said they were watching Enzo and would take care of him and my papa if I told anyone. A week later I forgot to put on all the makeup and ran into Tommy at the grocer. He saw all the bruises and pulled me out to his car. I begged him not to help me. I begged him to leave me alone because Roy was already angry with him for taking my virginity. But Tommy said he couldn't not help me. A month and a half later, the day after I graduated from high school, Tommy and I met up at Newark Airport. He sent me to Detroit after we opened a joint account. That's where I met with an attorney and had my name changed.

"I flew to Hawaii next and got settled, then six months later I started paying Tommy back. I don't know where he came up with fifteen grand, but I thanked him and we never talked again. I would put the money in the account using wire transfers through several banks that couldn't be traced, until this month when I got lazy. I used a branch in the Bronx near my apartment to transfer the money. That's how Roy must have found me. I didn't cover my tracks as good this month, and he already knew I was here. That's the only way he could have found me." I take a deep breath.

"You did good, dollface," Zeke says, and his lips touch my forehead.

Noah twists my body so I'm cradled against his chest.

"Baby." I look at him. "I'll protect you. Always." He buries his face into my neck and just holds me. And that's all I need right now. Knowing he's here for me.

"Kenzie?" Linc says my name quietly, breaking up the moment.

I shift but Noah doesn't let me off his lap.

"Before he starts, I'd like to say something, Kenzie," Jericho says. "I'm so glad I'm not your type and you and Noah found each other. I want you to be my little sister too and I'm here for you always." He reaches out his hand to me. I take it and nod at him.

I can't believe what any of the men are talking about. Noah says I'm his and they say I'm their little sister. I've been a little sister before and I sucked at it, but I pray I can be better for them, and I want this. I want Noah. I want the feelings of belonging and mattering again.

"Yes, Linc?" I look at him, ready for whatever question he's going to ask me.

CHAPTER EIGHT

NOAH

I hold her body close to mine, needing the contact. Everything she endured to be here and survived makes me want to kill Roy, but I'm humbled that she wants me too. I know she could have any man, even though I'd fight her on that. She's beautiful, intelligent, and strong. And all mine.

I know Linc needs to break down her story and confirm the details. Being on this side, I now understand what people go through when we question them. I don't want her to go through any more than she already has. I'm glad Zeke was able to get control of her because when she started to pull into herself, I didn't know what to do, but I'll be learning as I have a feeling my girl has had other panic attacks before. I wonder where my brother learned that technique.

"Kenzie, when was the last time you saw Roy Tramble?" Linc asks.

"I physically saw Roy in November when I went home to see my parents. When I saw him there, I knew I couldn't stay, so I ran. But I know he was at my apartment Friday night." She pauses and I wait for her to continue. "I've learned through the years how to be aware of everything around me. I was distracted Friday night when Noah took me home, and it wasn't until I walked up to my unit and saw the necklace that I knew." Again, another pause. "I ran out and jumped into an Uber, and that's when I realized I was being watched. He followed me all the way back into the city and I lost him somewhere in Times Square." She leans back into me, her body still so tense.

"What *family* does he work for?" He asks the question I've been wondering about since she mentioned it.

"I don't know." She shakes her head.

"Do you know the balance on the joint account?" he asks.

"Yes, I access it every month and would see the withdrawals, so somehow Roy got the information from Tommy."

She shivers and I nod at Jericho who jumps up and heads out of the room. When he returns moments later, he has my flannel that hangs in the closet by the door. He hands it to me, and I lean back so I can wrap her in it. She slips her arms through it and covers her little brown jacket with three-quarter sleeves. She pulls the collar to her face and sniffs and I almost groan at the image of my girl wanting to take in my scent. Her own scent was all that calmed me while she told her story.

"Where did Tommy get the money he gave you?" Linc continues with his questions.

"I don't know, and I never asked."

"Do you have any more questions?" Linc looks at me and I shake my head no.

"She's done for the night," I say as I twist her back around so her head is under my chin and I hold her close.

"I need to get back to my hotel. I have to work in the morning," she says and takes a deep breath as if she could fall asleep right here in my arms.

There is nothing in the world I want more than to hold her. To have her in my bed. But I know I need to give her time to understand what we are.

"Baby, we will get your stuff and you will be staying here. I know we can protect you here, I can't there."

She sits up and tries to pull herself from my lap, but I hold her tighter. She continues to struggle, and I look over her head.

"Let me go, Noah," she demands.

"Linc, get someone to watch her family. I'll make a phone call here in a moment. Zeke, we'll be ready to go in fifteen. Jer, are you coming?"

"Nope, I'll stay here," Jericho states as he stands and takes her plate into the kitchen.

Linc nods and I watch as he and Zeke make themselves scarce.

I lift her up and maneuver her body. "Open," I command and her legs spread so that she is straddling me. "Baby, I told you I'd protect you, and I can't do that with you there and me here." I bury my hands in her hair and tip her head back so she is looking at me. "I'm not going to have you away from me anymore. I told you the other night you weren't ready for what I wanted, but now you need to know. I want you. I want a chance to be with you. You are mine." Her eyes flare wide when I tell her she's mine.

"Noah, how? I want you and I to have a chance, but not until I get Roy taken care of." She bites her bottom lip and I'm instantly hard and needing her.

"No, now. I don't care about him. We will figure all this out."

I pull her face to mine, angling her head so I can take her mouth deep. Her eyes cloud with lust as she watches my lips get closer to hers. Just before I take her lips, her eyes close and her body relaxes into me. This is why she's mine.

My tongue sweeps into her mouth and I groan as she wraps her arms around me and smashes her breasts into my chest. Her long fingers slide through my hair and she rocks onto my hard cock. My tongue brands every part of her mouth, and as I pull away, I suck that full bottom lip into my mouth and gently bite it. She moans as her head falls back and I lean forward kissing and nipping her neck. Marking her with my teeth and scruff.

"Baby, if we continue this, I'm going to take you right here in our dining room. I don't won't our first time here. I want you in our bed, you under me begging for my cock as I kiss your pretty pussy." She grinds down on me harder and I realize my girl loves the dirty talk.

"Please, Noah," she begs.

"After we get back." I pull away and lift her up to stand next to me. I notice her legs are still trembling. "Come on." I pull her with me toward the back of the house where I see Zeke waiting in the garden. "Jer, we'll be back soon," I holler and he acknowledges.

I pull her in close to me after she grabs her bag and we head out to the detached garage. After I get her loaded into the back seat and Zeke is in the passenger, I dial the number of someone who can help us.

"Leave a message." Timothy's voice comes across the line and that's all.

"Dude, it's Noah. Call me, I need a favor." I hang up and hope he calls, if not I'll call the office in the morning.

"Going to get him to do some searches for you?" Zeke asks.

"Yeah, I want stuff I won't be able to get from work." I look in the rearview mirror and see my girl looking back at me. "Babe, what hotel?"

She names a run-down hotel in Times Square and I head that way.

"Who can do searches that the police can't?" she asks, and I knew she would clue into our convo.

"Baby, we need information that isn't in official reports. We need stuff about Roy that will get you safe. Got it? I will do everything in my power to keep you safe."

"Noah, you can't lose your job over this."

"I won't."

AFTER WE GET her stuff and check her out of the hotel, I take her home. She's never leaving here if I can help it. This is our home now. I knew when I was designing and working on this place it would be where the woman I fell in love with would live too, but the fact the house fits her perfectly shows me how fate has played a role in us. Before I take her upstairs to our room, I take her down to what was my man cave before I covered it in her plants.

"Oh my God, Noah." Her hand covers her mouth and she turns to me. Her gray eyes shine like silver as tears appear in them. I reach for her and fold my arms around her.

"I couldn't leave them there, and I knew you would want them. You put them wherever you want in the house or garden, this is your place now too."

"Noah." She sighs, and I've had enough.

I lift her over my shoulder and she giggles as I carry her up the two flights of stairs.

"Put me down, I can walk."

I smack her ass and push through the door to the master suite. Dropping her onto the bed, I look over and see that Zeke brought her bags here. She raises up on her forearms and sees them too.

"Noah, I'm not staying in here."

"Baby, you are staying here, and I'll sleep upstairs."

"I can't kick you out of your bed." She pushes up and I push her back. With my hand against her chest, I can feel her erect nipples through her clothing and my flannel.

"You will sleep in our bed until you're ready to share it with me. I told you this was your home, and it will be until the day we both pass."

I watch her take that in. She swallows slowly and then her fingers are in motion. She pulls my flannel and her jacket off. I reach down and pull off her little ankle booties and drop them on the floor behind me. She sits up and unbuttons the dress shirt I'm still wearing. Her tentative fingers are going too slow for me, so I push her hands away. I reach behind my neck and pull, lifting the shirt over my head, hearing it tear and not caring. I need her skin against mine.

She must feel the same way because she takes her T-shirt off and throws it across the room then falls back on the bed. Her breasts are barely contained in the blue lacy flowered bra. Her dusky nipples are erect and begging for my mouth. Her chest pulls in and out in large breaths. I tear my eyes from what I want and look up into her gray eyes. They're dark, almost a pale blue, and her perfect full bottom lip is between her teeth as she takes me in.

Slowly giving her the time to stop me, I lean down and press my chest into hers. She inhales and arches her neck back. I lick across her lips and she releases the bottom lip. It's rosy and shiny. I pull it into my mouth and bite it. She groans and follows me as I pull back away from her. Her head drops back to the bed and I look down at my woman. The woman I want to mark so every Tom, Dick, Harry, and Jughead knows she's mine. So Roy will leave her alone. I reach up and pull the band from her hair, letting her hair fall around her. My angel. Mine.

"Kenzie, tell me to stop now or I'm going to be buried deep inside you before long."

Her eyes cloud for only a moment then I watch them darken more. Her hands wrap around me and her little nails scratch down my back.

"I want you, Noah, but you're right, not tonight. Just kiss me and make me forget everything that has happened."

I lean forward and take her lips. The kiss drags on as I explore all of her. Her nails dig in and I slip my leg between hers and she starts rubbing on it. I groan from the contact and break from her lips.

I want to taste her more. I want to bury my face between her legs and breasts. I kiss down her neck and across her collarbone, down across the swell of her breasts. I pull a cup down under her breast and take the dusky nipple into my mouth, and swirl my tongue around it. Her back arches as she pushes more of her perfect breast into my mouth. I release it then give the other the same attention. I pull away and brush my chest against hers and the sound that comes from her mouth is more than I can stand. I push away from the bed and watch as she writhes in desire across it. I want to give her what she needs.

"Please, Noah, I need you," she begs.

"Baby, I want to, but you told me you wanted to wait. Let me help you and no more, okay?" It's going to be hard because I want her so much but for her, I'll do whatever she needs.

I reach down and undo her belt and pop the button of her jeans. I slide the zipper down and she watches everything I'm doing. Her pupils are dilated, the black blending into the gray. I slide her jeans down her legs and stand back to look at my girl. She's laid out on our bed, her breasts thoroughly loved, her nipples erect and turgid. Her blue bra pushing them up and on display with the cups pulled down. Her matching blue panties cover her mound but are soaked and the scent sets me on fire.

I pull the sides of her panties down over her toned, smooth thighs and drop them to the floor. Grabbing her ankles, I push them up on the bed close to her ass, then push her knees against her chest to open her up to me. I drop to my knees and praise God for the height of the bed. I lean in and swipe my tongue through her folds and softly circle her clit. She moans and I'm ready to ravish her. I open her with my fingers and lick, bite, and love her pretty little pussy. When I get to her opening, I thrust my tongue in like I want to thrust my cock into her. She cries out and arches off the bed trying to close her legs and move away from me. I wrap my arm around her and hold her to me while I attack her clit. I suck the little pearl into my mouth as she moans and thrashes more. I know she's close, so I keep her clit in my mouth and push two fingers into her tight heaven. She screams and comes on my face, and I want her to do it again. I pump my fingers into her and tease her clit some more.

"Please, Noah. Please. Oh God, Noah," she chants.

"One more, baby. Give me one more."

I rub my fingers against her G-spot and the scream that comes from her as she climaxes is music to my ears.

I look up. Her body is flushed with desire and I want to thump my chest. I did that to her. I rub my scruff against her more and she jerks from the sensitivity. I can't wait until I take her and claim her as mine.

I stand up and head for the bathroom where I get a cloth to clean her up. She barely moves or protests. I unhook the front clasp of her bra and help her out of it and then under the blankets. Watching her for a moment, I silently vow to protect her.

After I take a shower, where I relieve myself, I come out of the en suite bathroom to find her thrashing around on the bed in the throes of a nightmare. I slip on boxers and climb in next to her. She immediately quiets and curls into my body. I hold her close and kiss the top of her head.

CHAPTER NINE

KENZIE

I roll over and the feeling of soft sheets and being rested washes over me. I sit up so fast and try to place every-thing. I'm in a large room, the bed has a brown leather head-board, the comforter is a navy blue with white sheets.

"Fuck, baby, not that that isn't going to be my favorite sight, but if we are going to make it to work on time you better cover those," Noah says from the other side of the room.

I look over and see him standing in the doorway of the en suite bathroom. He's dressed in a blue suit today. The tie is a soft dove gray. Oh man, he's so hot.

"Babe, now," he says again, and I grab for the sheet to cover my breasts.

I look around for something to wear so I can get up when a T-shirt comes flying at me and lands at my side. It's the same black one from our date night. I slip it over my head and slide out of bed. I walk toward where my bags were last night, but they aren't there. I look around trying to find them.

"They're in the closet, babe. But first, come kiss your man so I can make breakfast while you're showering."

I walk to him trying not to feel awkward. I don't know what to do about last night. I want him and I want to see where this goes, but he's told me this is our house. Our room. I'm his. I feel claimed, not controlled like I did with Roy, and that's when I realize this is right.

I walk right into his arms and plaster myself against his chest. I lean up and peck his cheek. I don't want to kiss him with morning breath.

"Lips, babe," he growls, and I lean back with my hand over my mouth.

"Um, let me brush, please."

"Just kiss me."

I lean in and press my closed lips to his, and he wraps his arms around me, pulling me into him more. He pushes his tongue into my mouth, and I taste toothpaste and him. I moan and he deepens the kiss. He picks me up and turns us and sets me down inside the bathroom.

"Make yourself at home, baby. Meet me downstairs when you're ready."

He steps back and I watch him walk out of the bedroom. I almost swoon to the floor. Holy hell, batman! That was so hot.

I turn around and take in the huge room. The room is large, white and rock. There are no doors at either entrance. I walk through into a private parlor with a fireplace. The furniture is all cream colored and the floors are a hardwood with a large soft gray throw rug. There is a chaise lounge chair by the front windows and bookshelves line the walls again. On the fireplace mantle are pictures of his family and a beautiful woman I recognize but I don't know from where. I head back into the bathroom with the adjoining walk-in his and hers closets. I step into the one with my bags and open my suitcase to get out my uniform.

The shower has a seat with river rock embedded in the walls. My toiletries are already on the shelves, so I shower quickly and step out to grab a towel off the warming rack. When I walk up to the his and hers vanities, I notice that again my stuff is on the counter. He unpacked my things and I'm happy to see my toothbrush next to his. I finish getting ready and dressed.

When I walk down the stairs, I hear all the brothers in the kitchen and for a moment, I just stop and listen.

"I'll drop her off after I drop you off." Zeke's voice carries.

"I can drop her off and you both go to work," Jericho offers.

I step into the kitchen. "Boys, you don't need to fight, I'll take the train and it will be fine."

"Fuck no, baby. One of us will be picking you up or dropping you off," Noah says as he walks toward me.

He leans in and kisses me. Because my work shoes don't have heels, he has to lean down a bit more and I push up on my toes to meet him.

"Okay, you two, enough," Zeke growls, but I see the smile on his face when I look at him.

"Okay, Zeke and I'll take a cab, and you and Jericho can take my jeep."

"I get to drive." I bat my eyelashes at him, and he smiles down at me.

"Do you drive, baby?"

"Do I drive? I'm insulted, Mr. Caine. I drive very well. I drove around the island all the time instead of my roommate, Lysta. She hated to drive. Call her and ask if you don't believe me." I joke with him.

"I got this, she isn't driving." Jericho interrupts.

"I'm hurt." I cover my heart and act like I'm going to collapse.

Noah laughs and pulls me in close.

"Just let him drive, babe, you can drive Sunday when we go out to Mama's for dinner."

I instantly stiffen. Meet his mom. Oh hell no. His arms wrap around me and he leans down next to my ear.

"Relax, baby, she'll love you." He kisses my neck.

"I said enough. Don't make me spray you with water," Zeke grumbles again.

We laugh as Noah's phone rings. He pulls it out of his pocket and looks at the display, then hits the speaker button as he smiles.

"Caine."

"Hello, this is Bekah with Securities International. I was told to give you a call back." A female voice with a strange accent comes across the line.

"I was needing to speak to Timothy," Noah says as he stiffens and walks into the dining room.

I follow him and Zeke puts a plate of eggs and toast in front of me when I take a seat. I eat as I listen to the conversation.

"He's on leave for a bit and I'm taking over his duties. May I help you?" I can't place her accent, it's a combination of a couple different ones.

"I need a background check and search done, so only he can do it." Noah's impatience is coming out in his voice.

"Listen here, ya bloody yank, I can do just as much as Timmy boy can and better, so you just tell me what you need or ya figure it out on ya own." She blasts him through the phone, and a deep southern drawl comes across.

"Where is Timothy?" Noah asks again.

"That is none of your concern, Noah Caine, NYPD detective first grade with the 1st Division. Cold cases. Are you on the take because your bank account and investments are better than most cops?"

"Hey, how do you know that?"

"Let me see, I bet you'll hate it if I hack your accounts and send your money to charity." There's a pause over the line.

"Leave my money alone. I'm in the process of getting a new accountant since I lost my last one."

"Darn, you ruin all my fun. What can I help you with?"

"You're a hacker?"

"You're a bit daft, aren't ya?"

"Okay, I need a search on a Roy Tramble of New York, a full background."

"You can get that through your own resources, you don't need us."

"I do. I need things we won't look for, but you will. I needed Timothy to work his magic and check if my girlfriend is being searched."

"Name?" she asks.

"Yours first," he growls out.

"Like I said, I'm Bekah. Bekah Williams, computer technologist with Securities International. Now can I have your girlfriend's name?" She has a bite in her tone and I kinda like how she gives Noah issues.

"Kenzie Russo." He gives her my name, and again there's a brief pause.

"Nope, that's not her name. That name has only been in use for six years."

"Hey, you aren't supposed to be able to know that." I interrupt, too much money and documents were created to give me a full background.

"What're running from?" she asks.

I bite my lip trying to decide if I'm going to tell her everything. Noah's phone pings during the call and the video request chat lights up. He hits the button and we both look at the redhead with hair almost to her shoulders.

"I'm Bekah. Kenzie, it doesn't matter how good your background is, I can find you. Well, I can find most people. There are some that allude me. Background, please."

"Roy Tramble is my ex. He's threatened everyone I care about. I ran and changed my name."

"Well, now I know what to help you with. I see where you work. I need you to open an email I'm sending you when you get to work. I'm sending you a package right away. Should be there tomorrow. They're a pair of glasses. Wear them whenever you're not at home. They will distort any facial recognition software that is running on you. I've found your real name and I'll set up monitoring on your family. I'll hack their devices so we can have eyes on them."

"I can't allow you to send me an email at my work. I could lose my job if they found out I enabled a hacker to get into the system."

"No, girl. I'm doing this only to protect you. I could easily hack the NYPD on my own. I've done far worse. Whenever you go outside, wear your hair down and try to cover your face. Don't expose your ears. There is new search software that searches ears. I see there is already a track and trace set up on your identity and the following cell number." She rattles off my number and the panic starts to rise, thank goodness I shut it off.

"Fuck," Noah exclaims from beside me. "Bekah, have

they figured out where she is, and can you tell who is doing this?"

"I can see who the hacker is and I'm going to take care of them. I also altered his trace. I suggest new burner phones, and maybe turn on the old phone and fly it out of the country."

"Should I leave again," I ask, my heart dropping.

"No. I know the hacker, and they have some seriously good facial recognition software. Running is out of the option. Kenzie, can I just talk to you for a moment?" Bekah asks and I go to reach for the phone.

"Wait, anything you say to her I'd like to hear. I can't protect her if she has secrets from me," Noah says, and I can feel the tension coming off his body.

"I promise it will only be girl talk."

He hands over the phone and I head upstairs to the bedroom with my stomach in knots.

"Okay. I'm alone."

"I know about running and hiding. I've done it and I went up against Timothy. It took him a while to find me. Here are some suggestions. Don't use credit cards, even with your new identity. They know that one and so far haven't been able to find your employer. Remember the hair trick and use the glasses I'm sending you. I'll hack all the cameras in the neighborhood to be able to keep an eye on you. I'm going to talk to Noah about maybe bringing in some of the team to help you if he thinks it's time. I can talk to Maya and Joshua. Don't run. Trust he will protect you, okay?"

"Okay."

"You can rejoin Noah."

I walk back down to the dining room and Noah watches me carefully.

"Okay, Noah, I'm going to talk to the bosses and see

about getting you some help. You have two different mob families searching for your girl. One Roy hired, and the other is searching for her to go after Roy."

"Really? Fuck." Noah slides his hand through his short hair, and I can feel the irritation coming off him.

"If I wasn't so far into this pregnancy, I'd send my husband, Derek, but he won't leave my side right now at thirty-two weeks. Well, speak of the devil."

"Who are you talking to, Beks?" A deep voice comes across the line.

"Williams, is that you?" Zeke asks.

"Yeah, who is this?" Derek's face fills the screen.

"It's Zeke Caine. Your little missus was helping my bro here with his dollface."

"Damn, Caine, been a while. How is the DC area?"

"I'm in New York right now. Congrats, just heard your wife is expecting."

"Yeah, she needs to take a break for lunch now. What's going on?"

"I'll explain in a bit," Bekah says.

"Okay, we'll let you go, and thank you, Bekah," Noah says.

"Don't forget to open my emails," she says as she disconnects the chat.

"Is everything okay, baby?" Noah asks as I pace.

"No, it's not okay. Two mob families are looking for me and now you want to introduce me to your mother. I'm not ready for this. I can't." I turn and head for the garden when strong arms twist me around and I'm thrown over his shoulder.

Noah carries me through the house, up the stairs, and into his room. He slams the door shut and propels me through the air to the bed. He lands on top of me and cages me in with his body.

"We don't have time for me to show you properly what your running does to me. But know this right now, baby. Every time you try to run from me, you will end up right back here under me. I'll fuck your need to run from me out of you. Do you understand?" He grits out just before his mouth lands on mine.

His lips claim my submission and I open for him. His tongue tangles with mine, and I wrap my arms and legs around him and pull him closer. I grind myself against him. Needing the connection.

He rips his lips from mine. We are both panting from our desire. "Fuck, baby, I can't wait to claim that sweet little pussy of yours. But right now, I'm going to work with a serious case of blue balls, and you are going to work knowing I'm never letting you go."

"Noah." I sigh his name in desire and worry.

"Kenzie, we will figure this out. As for my mother, I told you she will love you. Uncle Romeo has already called me a few times trying to get us to come back and have dinner. Which we are doing on Friday. Now, let's get up and get out of here."

He stands up and I can make out his erection pushing against his slacks. I lick my lips, wanting this to continue and not focusing on the fact we are going to be running late soon.

"Babe," Noah growls. "Eyes up here or we will both be calling in sick."

I raise my eyes, startled that the command in his voice affects me by causing my womb to spasm and desire to dampen my panties. I've never had this reaction to a man.

"Noah, I'm..." I don't know how to tell him.

He reaches out to me and without thought, I take his hand and he pulls me up to him.

"I'm here, Kenzie. I'm ready to give you everything I am and I'll guide you through this. I've never wanted a woman like I want you," he confesses as his hands slide down my body and cup my ass cheeks.

The image of the woman whose picture is on his mantle flashes in my mind.

"Really?"

"Yes, really."

"You've never been with anyone else or desired them?" I ask dumbfounded.

"I never said that, baby. What I said is, I've never wanted a woman as much as I want you. Why do you ask?" He tips his head to the side and arches an eyebrow.

"I saw that woman's picture in the sitting room. I recognize her but I don't know how."

"Oh, Kat. Um..." He starts to pull away and I'm worried now.

I bite my top lip and look down, hoping to hide the hurt.

"Baby, don't be jealous of her. For one, she was my best friend. Yes, we dated, but she and I made much better friends than lovers. Someday I'll explain more, but know this, Kathryn is gone, and if she were alive, she'd adore you and try to corrupt you."

"She's gone?" I ask and look up at him.

His hand cups the side of my face.

"She died several months ago. And the reason you probably recognized her is because she was a model."

"Oh my goodness! She was that world-famous model killed in China." I can't believe he knows someone that famous, but I can imagine him being with that beautiful of a woman, and I feel lacking.

"Baby, you need to know when Kat and I were together was a long time ago. Yes, I used to think we'd get back together, but since I've laid eyes on you, I realized she was always right. She wasn't the woman for me. You're the woman I want. You are beautiful, strong, and all mine."

He reassures me and I lift up to kiss him. His arms pull me in tight and we continue to kiss until we hear the yell.

"I told you I'd throw water on you two. Now come on, we got work," Zeke yells from right outside the door.

We both laugh and he leads me to the door firmly holding my hand in his strong one.

When we get downstairs, Jericho is waiting by the back slider and Zeke is by the front door.

"Okay, baby, don't go anywhere without Jericho. Remember what Bekah suggested. I'll meet you here tonight and we'll order some food. Okay?"

"Okay," I say, and he pulls me close and kisses my forehead. "Be careful. Both of you." I look around Noah to Zeke. Doing their jobs is dangerous and I know that.

As I turn to walk away, Noah swats my ass.

"Remember, baby, I'll come after you," he growls when I turn back around.

"I know."

I head out with Jericho.

CHAPTER TEN

KENZIE

"Hey, girl, are you there?"

Trina's voice breaks through the fog of desire. All I can think about is what will happen tonight. I want Noah. I want him more than I've ever wanted a man, and all I can imagine is him taking me.

"Hey, Keni, you're blushing." She laughs, and I realize I'm flushed from the images.

"Um, sorry. How are you?" Both of us have been so busy we haven't been able to talk at all today.

"Besides busy worried about you. Are you sure you're safe and okay with him?"

I chuckle at her concern. "You set us up, remember?" She laughs again. "I'm safe with him, and yes, I'm okay. I like him, like him in a way I haven't liked anyone in a while. But I'm worried about him. And he makes me feel things I never expected to feel so soon."

"Sounds like that's good then."

"Yeah, it is."

Our monitors go crazy again and I only get to tell her goodbye before she takes off.

Finally, my shift is over and I wait in the lobby until I see Jericho pull up out front. I head out and climb into the jeep.

"Hey, sis, how was your day?"

"Good. Can we stop at the grocer before we go to the house? I want to grab some food."

"Okay."

After a quick shopping trip, I change into a pair of denim cutoff shorts and a navy shirt. Barefoot, I'm in the kitchen working on making a nice dinner for the guys. I know Noah doesn't have normal hours, but I texted him from the grocer and he said he'd be home in about an hour. That gives me time to make my chicken piccata and lemon garlic broccoli. Jericho assured me there wasn't anything they didn't like.

I've got my music pumping through my speaker. Halestorm's "Beautiful with You" comes on and I'm dancing and singing around the kitchen to it. Arms wrap around me and I instantly go on the defensive trying to fight them off until I smell his cologne and calm.

"Shit, Noah, you scared the crap out of me," I exclaim as his hands slide up the underside of my shorts, his thumbs so close to my core.

"Baby, don't ever wear these out of the house or I'll shred them," he growls as he kisses my neck.

"Noah." I pant until I smell the chicken. "Stop distracting me or dinner will burn." I try to pull away.

"Fuck, you barefoot in our kitchen gives me lots of ideas. All of them include you under me and us alone."

"Stop." I giggle, and he pulls away.

"What are you making, sexy?"

"Chicken piccata." I smile at him.

"That sounds good. Let me change and I'll be down in a sec to help you finish."

"I just need the table set and the wine poured."

"Okay."

He takes off and I finish adding the capers to the pan. He's back fast and has the table set and a white wine poured for us. He hollers for Jericho, who comes up from downstairs.

"Shit, dude, if you don't want her, I do. She cooks too."

Noah smacks him in the back of the head and the pushing starts.

"She's mine. Find your own."

"Sit down, both of you," I order as I hear the front door open.

"Damn, not only does it smell like Mama's, but it sounds like it too," Zeke states as he walks into the dining room. "Yum, you cooked? Just a sec." He takes off his jacket, tie, and rolls up his sleeves.

We settle in for a fun dinner getting to know each other. Afterward Jericho offers to clean up, and Noah grabs my glass of wine and refills it before dragging me from the room.

We end up upstairs on a small balcony off the bedroom. It overlooks the garden below. The sounds of New York can be heard, but right here in the small area I feel like we are alone. We sit on a large white and brown outdoor sectional and he pulls me toward him. I cuddle into his body and instantly relax. It's perfect.

"I know tomorrow is your day off and I hope you'll stick around here for the day."

"I need to get my plants moved around and taken care of. I was also going to work in your garden for the day. Is that okay?"

"Baby, that's your garden now. If you want to add anything to it or change it, we can."

I push up and look down at him. "Noah, you can't be serious. Right now, I'll pretend it's mine, but some day you'll get tired of my drama and want someone who doesn't have all this baggage—"

Before I can complete my sentence, I'm on my back and he's over the top of me. His large body pins me down.

"What did I tell you earlier? What do I keep telling you?"

"That I'm yours and this is my home now."

"That's for fucking real, baby."

He leans down and kisses me softly. He lays back and again we are just relaxing.

"Do you like dogs?" he asks me after a few moments, breaking the quiet.

"Yes. Why do you ask?"

"I have a friend who trains dogs and he's been bugging me for a while to come get one of his. I think I need to get one for you, to protect you."

"But, Noah, we both work so much."

"It'll be okay. We'll make it work. Come on." He stands up and holds out his hand. I take it and he pulls me up to him and then up into his arms. He carries me into the room and lays me on the bed. "All night I've been trying not to drag you up here and take these shorts off you. Now show me what you have on under these sexy-as-fuck shorts," he growls and my core spasms.

I sit up and pull my T-shirt over my head, leaving me in my low-cut white push-up bra. His breath hitches and I toss the shirt at him. He catches it and throws it toward the corner where the hamper is. I pop the button of my shorts and unzip them. Then I shimmy them down my hips as I flex my hips up.

"Fuck this." He grabs my shorts and pulls them down my legs.

I lie there feeling a little uncomfortable as he just stares at me.

"You are sexy as fuck," he says, then reaches behind his neck and pulls the shirt over his head, tossing it toward the hamper too.

When he pops the first button of his jeans, I see the ruddy head of his penis peeking out. He's commando under them and I bite the side of my lip. My breathing increases, and I watch as his erection gets harder and more of it peeks out. When the pearly drop of pre-cum glistens on the tip, I've waited enough. I sit up and raise my eyes to his.

"I want to taste you," I say, knowing he wants to control this.

"Fuck." He steps back from the bed and I slide off and kneel in front of him.

I don't want to waste any of him, so I snake my tongue out and lick up the drop. I moan as his flavor bursts on my tongue. I pop the rest of the buttons on his jeans and pull them partway down his legs. His cock is long and thick, the tip is red and now glistens from the pre-cum and my tongue. I want another taste.

I lick up his cock from root to tip, swirl my tongue around the tip and back down. I do that a couple more times until I notice the thick muscles in his legs tightening. Wrapping my hand around the base, I slip him into my mouth and moan as more of his pre-cum slips across my tongue. He pulls the hair tie from my head and my curls fall down my back.

I look up him as I suck him into my mouth again. His eyes are nearly brown in his desire for me. His mouth is open, and he moans, his stomach muscles are tight. With my other hand, I reach up and drag my nails down his body and the top of his thigh, and his head falls back. I gently fondle his heavy balls in my hand.

"Fuck, stop," he growls as I swallow the head of his cock down my throat.

I slip off and slide him back in and swallow again. He growls as he comes down my throat. I swallow his cum and moan at the taste.

He grips me under my arms and lifts me off his cock. "I said stop, baby, and when I say that from now on, you'll listen to me. Now I'm going to fuck this pussy and claim it as mine for always."

"Yes, please, Noah," I beg.

My thong is ripped from my body and I writhe on the bed wanting him in me. I slide my hands into the cups of my bra and pull my breasts out as I pinch my nipples. Biting my lip, I try to find the relief my body demands.

"Stop trying to force it, baby. I'm going to make you come so hard you'll scream my name so the whole neighborhood knows you're mine."

He pushes me up on the bed and he's between my legs naked. He strokes his still hard cock and I realize he didn't fully come.

"I'm clean, baby, tell me I can have you bare."

"I'm clean and I'm on the shot."

He lifts my legs over his arms and raises my ass up to him. He thrusts his tongue into me like I want his cock.

"Please," I beg.

He lowers my ass back down but doesn't release my legs. He pushes the head of his cock into my entrance slowly and pulls out, repeating his actions, going deeper each time. Finally, when he's completely seated inside me, he drops forward over my body, almost bending me in half. His mouth takes one of my nipples and he gently bites it. I can't move very much as he starts moving in and out of me. He moves faster and I feel the edges of a powerful orgasm. It's going to consume me and I'm scared. I raise my eyes to his instead of watching his cock penetrate me.

"Let go, baby, I've always got you."

And like my body was waiting for permission, I come, and the colors burst around me. My breathing staggers in my lungs. My legs spasm and my scream is so loud I know his brothers heard me. But he doesn't stop, he continues to push his way into my body. Dominating me and causing the orgasm to continue rolling through my body. I whip my head back and forth. My nails dig into the muscles of his arms as he takes me for another orgasm, even bigger than the last. My eyes roll back, my neck extends, and over my screams of his name, I hear him yell my name.

He releases my legs and his elbows land next to my head. His body holds me down and we both are trembling from the aftershock. My breathing isn't normal yet, but he rolls to the side sliding out of my body, and the separation feels as if I've lost a part of me. He continues to roll until he's flat on his back and pulls me on top of him. I lay my head on his chest and listen to his heart thumping under my ear. He unhooks my bra and I slide my arms out of the straps as he pulls it off then tosses it toward the pile of clothes.

"Baby, let's go take a shower."

"Hmm." I agree, and he sits up with me still on him.

"Wrap your legs around me."

I do as he says, and he carries me into the bathroom. He reaches in while one hand holds my ass. When he steps in instead of letting me down, he sits on the bench.

I unfold my legs so I'm straddling him. He pulls my head

up, one hand under my chin, the other knotted in my hair at the back of my head.

"Kenzie, I've told you before, but now you need to understand there is no going back. You are mine. I've never had a sexual experience like that before and I'm pretty sure you haven't either. I'm never letting you go." He pulls me to him, and his tongue is in my mouth taking everything from me.

I feel him harden again and I shift against his cock wanting him again. He's right, I've never felt this before. I don't have a lot of experience, but what I do was nothing like what just happened.

He shifts me and impales me on his cock. "I can't get enough of this tight little pussy of yours." He groans as he waits for me to accommodate to his size.

I flex my knees and proceed to move over him. His hands cup my breasts and he pinches my nipples, causing me to spasm and both of us to groan. I continue to ride his cock and when I twist, he hits a deeper spot inside me.

His hand leaves my breast and holds my waist, where he guides me to move my body over him again and again slowly. His other hand continues to play with one nipple. I look in his eyes, seeing things in them that scare and thrill me at the same time.

I wasn't looking for someone, but now that I have him, I'm never letting him go.

"If I'm yours..." I pant. "Then you're mine." I grit out, trying to hold off the orgasm I'm now feeling, and I stutter in my thrusts slightly.

Both of his hands are on my waist and he starts moving now. He pulls me down as he flexes up into me.

"Oh God."

He leans forward and bites my neck. "I'm not God, baby. I'm Noah, your man. Now say my name," he demands as he thrusts harder and I brace my hands on his shoulders, using his body to help me.

I lean into him, which causes him to rub against my clit, and that's all I need to detonate screaming his name as he groans mine. Again, I feel him throb and come inside me.

"Someday, baby, I'm going to put my baby in your little belly and you're going to love it."

"Yes." I sigh as we sit on the bench with the steam filling the shower around us.

When he stands and slides out of me again, I feel a slight pain from tender muscles and the loss again.

We clean each other up and dry each other off. When we climb into bed, I curl naked into his body and fall asleep after I kiss him good night. With his arms around me, I've never felt so safe and content.

CHAPTER ELEVEN

NOAH

I can't help myself. I can't get enough of her. I proceed to wake her up several times during the night and make love to her until she screams my name every time. As I slip into her tight little pussy early in the morning, I wish she wasn't using protection and we had made a baby with all our lovemaking.

I make slow love to her this time. Showing her how much she means to me. This time when she goes to scream, I take it in me as I kiss her. When I pull out and slide out of bed, I wash her with a cloth, and she cuddles into my pillow falling back to sleep.

"Sleep, beautiful. I'll call you on my lunch break."

She doesn't say anything, just mumbles, and I laugh as I get ready for work.

All day I've been distracted by thoughts of Kenzie. I haven't gotten her a burner phone yet, so Jericho has been messaging me updates when I bug him.

Jericho: She's on her laptop on some message board with a guy.

This is news to me, so I call him.

"Who is it?"

"Well, I didn't ask because I'm not going to invade her privacy like that." He smarts off.

"Give her your fucking phone, jackwagon," I demand.

"Hello." Her sweet voice comes across the line.

"Baby, who are you talking to online? Remember you need to stay off the web."

"I know, but without my phone, I can't get messages on my family. This is a secure board for finding long lost family members and loved ones. It's how Marco found me in Hawaii."

"Fuck, I'll get a phone for you that has the same number but a different sim card."

"Oh my God. I gotta go."

She hangs up the phone on me and I immediately dial it back and get no answer. Fuck.

I open the email from Bekah and click on the link I should have yesterday. I respond to her email, telling her Kenzie might be running. An instant message window pops up. I know Bekah has access to the cameras around my house, so she will know what's going on better than anyone.

Bekah: She's heading toward your auto. Your brother is chasing her now.

Noah: Where are they going? She was on some board for lost loves checking on her family.

Bekah: I'll look, just a moment.

"Hey, Noah, I just heard from someone I know in Brooklyn that Enzo Graco was shot about twenty minutes ago," Linc says, breaking through my fog of worry.

"Shit, let's go." I jump up.

Linc and I head out, and even with lights and sirens running we are still held up. When we pull up, I see Kenzie and Jericho running into the emergency entrance. She's in ripped up jeans and a tank top.

"Kenzie," I yell, and she stops and turns.

The look of devastation on her face is so hard to see. She runs for me and I grab her close when she's within arm's reach.

"Fuck, baby. You can't run off like this. This is probably a trap to get to you." I notice she does have on a pair of sunglasses and her hair is down.

"I don't care. I need to see him, this is my fault."

She cries in my neck and I hold her tight. When I set her down on her nude high heels, she wobbles slightly, and I know it's from her worry. My guess is she grabbed the first pair of shoes she could get her hands on before she ran out the door.

I hold her hand tight and we all walk into the ER entrance. Sitting in the main area is her family and her mother's gasp has Kenzie pausing. She doesn't pause for long, she doesn't care anymore, and I'm so proud of my girl. She walks right into her mother's waiting arms and they cling to each other.

"I'm so sorry. This is my fault. I'm so sorry." Kenzie repeats over and over.

Her father now has his arms wrapped around both women and he is crying too. They are all at a loss right now. On one hand they finally have their daughter in their arms, but on the other, their son is back behind those doors being treated and no one knows how bad it is. I stand back and wait. Her brother Marco notices me and walks over to me.

"You knew she was my sister before you came to question us. What is your game, Caine?" he yells and everyone stops.

"No game. I didn't know for sure until I saw her picture. Her name is different than yours." I try to explain but I can tell it's not working. His fists are flexing and he's shaking out his arms. I get it, he's upset about his brother and he's going to take it out on me.

"So now you're fucking her—"

I'm on him instantly and I feel Jer step up close, his hand on my shoulder.

"Whoa there, Noah." Jericho holds me back from slugging him.

"Listen here, you fuck, if you ever say that statement around me again in regard to your sister, I won't think twice, I'll knock you the fuck out."

"Marco, stop," Kenzie yells as she pushes him back and gets between us.

"Kenzie, baby, step back by Jer now." I grit out as I watch her brother's eyes harden, the gray turning almost black.

"Baby? What are you to her? How do you know her? Did you take advantage of her?" he demands and I'm about to lay him out, but Kenzie won't move. She wraps her arms around me and holds me close to her, but she won't move out of the way.

"Kenzie." I grit out again, but she ignores me.

"You listen here, Marco. Noah and I met only the night before he questioned you. We didn't know the connection. But now he's my..." She pauses, trying to figure out what I am to her.

"I'm her fucking boyfriend, her man, so you better watch how you speak about her because I don't need a badge to kick your ass."

"Yeah, he's my boyfriend, and I'll kick your ass myself if

you disrespect him again." Kenzie continues and I wrap my arms around her. One across her shoulders and the other across her stomach. The hold is possessive and will also allow me to push her to Linc or Jer if her brother decides not to stop.

"How did he not know he was interrogating your family?" Marco demands.

"I told you, I didn't know until I saw her picture."

"But her name?" Marco starts pulling on his longer hair.

"My name isn't Graco anymore," Kenzie says as her parents both gasp in surprise. "I had my name legally changed after I ran so Roy couldn't find me."

"Kenzie, you gotta think this is fucked up. He's investigating you for murder," Marco implores and her parents just stand back and watch. Her mother silently crying still.

"I'm not under investigation. I'm in protective custody," she explains. "Roy is coming after me." She finishes and her family all step back.

"Family for Graco," is called by a nurse and we all turn. "This way." She directs, and we all follow. Linc and Jer wait in the lobby.

We head down the hall toward the private rooms. She directs us through the large trauma room, and we all stand and wait for the doctor. Sitting on the bed with his arm bandaged and shirtless is Lorenzo Graco, Enzo.

When he sees Kenzie, he goes to stand up but a small woman in a black suit pushes him back down. Her back is to me, so I don't know who it is, but she has a lot of hair up in a tight bun on the back of her head. Her hands are covered in black latex free gloves. When she turns, I see the flash of her shield and recognize the face as she closes the case on the tray next to his bed.

"Sit the fuck down, asshole, before you tear those

stitches they just put in you." Her thick Jersey accent is thicker the longer she talks, and I know she's angry.

"Why don't you get the fuck out of here, Ryzer. You got your bullet. Go look in a fucking microscope." Enzo looks at her with the full force of his glare as he sits up higher in the bed.

"Lorenzo Salvatore Graco, you don't talk to women that way." Sal raises his voice and I watch the play of emotions across Enzo's face. Something about this woman bothers him.

"It's okay, this Graco has no manners. The doc will be back in a moment," she says as she winks at Marco, flirting with him, and he smiles back.

Enzo growls something I can't hear. She strips off her gloves and picks up her case then makes her way toward me.

"Hello, Detective Inspector Ryzer," I greet her. "Hey, can you compare that bullet with the others from my case?"

"Hey, Caine, yeah I can do that. I'll expedite my results as fast as I can. Smack him around a bit for me, please. This big fucker is constantly giving me shit." She shakes my hand when she walks by me and out of the room.

I laugh after her because Ryzer doesn't put up with anyone giving her shit. They end up on their ass when she kicks it. She is also one of the best crime scene investigators I've worked with, and her gun and bullet knowledge rivals the FBI's techs.

"Sis," Enzo groans, and Kenzie drops my hand and walks to him. He pulls her in for a one-armed hug.

Finally, Marco hugs her too before she returns to my side.

"Do you know what happened?" I ask, the cop in me demanding to ask questions.

"It was that asshole Roy. I caught a glimpse of the same

car he was in when he came by our house months ago. I saw him too."

"Fuck. Oh sorry, ma'am," I say, turning to Mrs. Graco.

"These three men are always cussing, so go ahead, young man. Why is Kenzie in danger?"

"Roy is after me to get me back, but he threatened you guys too. I've tried to stay away, but when Papa had his heart attack, I had to come home."

"Keni, you should have told us," her father says as he takes her in his arms again.

"I couldn't. I would have run again if not for Noah and the fact I'm tired of running."

"So, did he kill Tommy?" Enzo asks me.

"We're not sure yet but we should know soon. It's looking like it, though. I'm going to have you all put in protective custody to keep you safe."

"No," everyone says at once except Kenzie.

"Please, I can't lose you. We're lucky Roy missed this time," she begs.

"Baby, he didn't miss." I start to offer my theory. "This was his way of getting you out into the open so he can follow you."

"Fuck," Marco says.

"How are you going to get her out of here, Caine?" Enzo asks, trusting me.

"I have some ideas, but she isn't going to like them." I smile at her.

"I know how to evade him. I've been doing it for years," she says.

I pull her into my arms. "Now it's my turn. I'm good at this. I've got Bekah on speed dial and we're going to play a game of cat and mouse with him."

"You're going to use my daughter as bait," Sal growls.

"No, sir, I would never use her that way. But we are going to send him on a wild goose chase."

"I'm good. I'll be out of here in a bit, so you get her out of here now."

"I can't leave," Kenzie argues as she pulls from my arms and goes to her brother again. "I did this."

"Yes, you can, Keni. Get over there with your man and do what he says. And no, you didn't do this, fucking Roy did this."

She hugs everyone goodbye and we head out to the lobby.

"Hope you have a plan because this was a trap," Linc says as we rejoin him, and I nod at him.

"Jer, take the jeep back to your station, we'll pick it up after dinner. Then take a cab to the house after you confirm you're not being followed.

"On it. Be careful." He chucks Kenzie on the chin and nods at Linc and I before he takes off.

"Okay, Linc, you're going to take us in the squad car, and we are going to give this fucker the slip."

We head out to the parking lot and this time I take in my surroundings. The hair on the back of my neck rises. He's here.

We've only been on the road a few minutes when we stop at a stoplight and I jump out and open the back door, letting Kenzie out. I take her hand and we take off down the stairs for the subway. When we jump on the first subway pulling up, I know he won't be able to follow us onto it, but he can wait down the line. So at the next station, we stay on and jump off at the next, jumping onto the opposite train and heading back the way we came. We head further into Brooklyn and away from Manhattan. After a couple more train switches, we climb up to the street level and jump in a cab, but only take that to the edge of Manhattan where we get off in the Financial District. We walk around while I call Bekah and have her do a search of the area, then we get into another cab and head home.

When we step into the hall, I breathe a sigh of relief.

"Go get changed for dinner. Zeke is meeting us at the restaurant in an hour." I swat her ass as she turns toward the stairs.

She turns back and kisses me hard. I take the kiss to the next level and want to take her upstairs and show her how I feel about her being in danger, but I don't because my phone pings in my pocket. I pull it out and see the text from Linc.

Linc: He followed me into the district but I lost him before I got to the station.

Noah: Okay. We have dinner at Uncle's tonight. Are you coming?

Linc: No, I'll see you Monday. I'm on my way to pick up Samantha now.

Noah: Okay, give the little squirt hugs from Uncle Noah.

CHAPTER TWELVE

KENZIE

I enter the room and decide I need to take a quick shower to wash off the dirt from working in the garden earlier. I don't wet down my hair but afterward I flat iron it smooth. I wear my wrap maxi dresses in a floral print with a pair of black four-inch high heels that lace up my ankle.

I wish I had seen Roy today and we could have ended it, but I know Noah wouldn't want that. I'm glad Bekah's package came with the glasses in it. Two pairs, one for sunny days and one for not. It also had a few bangle style bracelets that the note said to never take off. I slip them on. Three are solid with cubic zircons in them, and the last is a chain style one. I know they have some kind of trackers in them and for everyone, I will wear them.

I grab a lightweight jacket and head downstairs. It's been thirty minutes and I know we have fifteen minutes of travel time, so I'm not going to make us late.

When I step down onto the main floor, I don't hear anyone and realize the guys are downstairs in Noah's man cave. I walk down the stairs and when I hear Noah's exclamation, I know I look good.

"Fuck, baby. How about we cancel and eat in, just you and me?"

"Your brother owes you dinner for losing, so we are going. Besides, I want to see your uncle again."

"But, baby, you look too good to go outside," he begs as he walks over to me.

"I wouldn't take a girl looking that good around Uncle Romeo. He might steal her." Jericho pipes in with a chuckle and heads upstairs. He's dressed in slacks and a black Henley. He really is cute but he's just not my type.

Noah takes me into his arms and leans down to my ear. "When we get home, I'm going to fuck you against the wall of our parlor with you in this dress and heels."

My breath hitches and I bite my bottom lip. He pulls it from between my teeth and kisses me.

"Noah, my lipstick." I pull away, but he runs his thumb around my lips, sweeping the smeared color off.

I use my hand to wipe it off his lips and we head upstairs to find Jericho has a cab waiting for us. I slip on the regular glasses and step out of the house and down the stairs. Jericho sits in front and I slide into the back with Noah next to me. His dark gray suit with a white shirt stretches across his muscled body as he pulls me close. He has one arm across my shoulders and the other hand is sitting on my thigh, gently stroking my leg in the open of the wrap.

I tighten my legs, trying to relieve the pressure on my clit from the desire to have him touch me. Before I know it, we are pulling up to the restaurant and standing out front is Zeke.

"Hey, you didn't go in?" Jericho asks.

"No, the new hostess wouldn't take her eyes off me, so I stepped out here."

"Well at least it's you and not me anymore," Noah says and I remember her from last time.

I take his hand and when we step into the darkened interior, I see her and I'm immediately jealous. Unable to hold it back, I turn and plaster myself against the front of Noah and wrap my arms around his neck.

"What's up, baby?" he asks, and I pull his head down to me, claiming him in front of her.

I hear the chuckles around us but it's the gasp that has me smiling and pulling away. Again, I wipe my lipstick off his lips and look into his hazel eyes that have darkened with desire.

"Yep, we should have stayed home," he whispers.

"Nope. I'm perfectly happy to be out now." I smile as I turn around to head to the back of the restaurant where Uncle Romeo is waiting for us.

"Oh no, you don't," Noah growls as he grabs my hand, pulling me back to him, and kisses me again.

This time it's all tongue and I must admit I do want to go back home with him.

He pulls away and then whispers in my ear. "Now that's how you lay a claim, baby." He leads me away from the entrance and I follow along, trying to collect myself and my raging hormones.

"Hello, *bellissima*. I see you and Noah have made up," Romeo says.

I lean in so he can kiss my cheek.

"Yes, sir. He told my family today he was my boyfriend." I smile at him.

"Is that all? Because the show I just saw looks like you two are a little more than that." He chuckles.

"Uncle Romeo, as soon as I can convince her, she will have my ring on her finger and my name." Noah pipes in as he helps me sit.

I swing my head to look at him in shock. Did he just say that? Does he want to marry me? He said I was his. Damn it, why do I keep questioning him on this?

He sits next to me and Romeo sits on my other side.

"You're eating with us?"

"Why yes, *bellissima*, I couldn't turn down having dinner with such a captivating beauty. Oh, and my nephews too." He gestures toward them and I laugh.

We have a fun evening with them sharing stories and good food. As the night comes to an end, Uncle Romeo, as I'm supposed to call him now, hugs me goodbye but whispers in my ear.

"Don't doubt your heart, *bellissima*. He will guard and protect it with his own. These men are like their father, they know who they are meant to be with as soon as they see her. And you, my darling, are Noah's heart." He kisses my cheek again and as we head out, the hostess makes a snide comment, but Uncle Romeo hears her.

"You can leave right now. Tomorrow I will decide if you can return."

The girl huffs and turns to walk to the back of the restaurant. I feel bad she is possibly being let go, but she shouldn't have said anything, and she really shouldn't have kept pushing herself on Noah after he told her once he wasn't interested.

Noah and I head back to the house while Jericho and Zeke go get Noah's jeep and bring it home.

Just like Noah said he would, he fucks me against the bookshelves in the parlor of the master suite. He lifts my skirt, rips my panties off, and fucks me hard.

E.M. SHUE

I scream his name several times before he helps me out of the dress, and we make love again on the chaise lounge.

"Baby, I can't get enough of you," he confesses while on his knees in front of me in the shower as I sit on the bench.

"Oh, Noah, I'm going to come again." I moan as he sucks my clit into his mouth and two of his fingers are buried in my pussy.

I scream as he reverses our positions, but with me on top of him and his cock buried deep inside me. Just like the night before, we make love again and again, all night long.

The next morning, I wake to his arms wrapped tightly around me as he spoons behind me. I quietly slip from his arms and the bed and go downstairs after dressing in sweatpants and one of his T-shirts.

I don't hear anyone else moving around, so I start cooking breakfast. I had some groceries delivered the day before and decide that pancake, bacon, and eggs would wake the guys up.

I'm not sure what the plans are for today, but I need to work out and I need to move more of my plants around, I already put a few upstairs in our rooms and was going to put some up here on the main floor. I also want to work in the garden some more. I have a few ideas of plants I want to bring in.

The bacon is cooked, pancakes are started, and I'm waiting to start the eggs when I hear feet on the stairs.

"If that's bacon, I'm marrying her and he can go find someone else," Jericho yells through the house.

"You take my woman and they won't find your body, asshole," Noah says as all three of them skid to a stop at the entrance to the kitchen.

I look over my shoulder at the three brothers. Of course, I have eyes only for my man, but the three of them together,

114

with their hair mussed from sleep, and unshaven, is a sight any woman would drool over.

"Damn, dollface, but you're a part of this family permanently because you make breakfast," Zeke growls as he walks to the coffee pot and pours himself a cup.

"I'm going to email my bestie back on the island and have her send us some island blends, but I got French roast, if that's okay?" I ask.

Noah walks over to me and wraps his arms around my body. "Baby, us not having to cook makes our day." He kisses the side of my neck and sniffs my hair, something I'm still getting used to.

Noah said he loved the smell of my tropical shampoo. I didn't tell him I had to order it and have it shipped to me because they were products sold by a Hawaiian company.

I have all my hair piled up on my head because after our shower last night, I didn't get to blow it out. So, all the waves and curls have taken over.

After breakfast Noah tells me to change into jeans and a shirt. I'm now standing here waiting to see where we are going in my distressed blue jeans, a blue button-down shirt, and brown high-heeled boots. I have my sunglasses on while I look at the garden waiting for Noah to get off the phone with Linc.

There's something going on and he doesn't want me to know. As he hangs up and walks out to me, I see the worry on his face, the pinched brow, the veins popping out across his neck. He's stressed.

"What aren't you telling me?" I ask him as I slip my arms around his waist and look up into his face.

"Not right now. I want you to enjoy your weekend. Come on, baby."

"Is it my family?"

"No, they're safe. We've convinced your parents to have protective custody but your brothers won't. Now, come on."

He pulls away and takes my hand, and leads me to the garage where we load up into his jeep. He heads out and crosses over into Jersey heading south. His hand rests on my thigh and I feel him tense as he thinks through whatever is bothering him.

"Please tell me, Noah. The not knowing is worse."

"I know, baby, but I don't want you to worry."

"What did Roy do now?"

He pauses and his hand flexes again. I watch as the muscles tighten in his body.

"Promise me you trust me?"

"Of course."

"The guy named Gino that I guess Trina tried to set you up with was found murdered this morning in Queens."

"What! Oh my God. Noah, we need to turn around. You need to find him and stop him before he hurts more people," I beg as tears roll down my face.

How can we be out on a drive and him not care?

"Baby, I'm not on the case until they have proof he was killed by Roy. Right now, they are going through the evidence, and Monday we should have ballistics back on your brother's shooting. Now please, we need to go do this, so just relax."

"What? What are we doing?" I throw his hand off my leg and fold my arms across my chest.

"We are getting you a dog for protection."

"I don't want a dog. I have a gun. I know how to fight and I'm tired of this. Use me as bait. He'll come after me and you can get him."

Noah yanks the wheel and pulls off to the side of the Garden State Parkway onto the shoulder. He puts the jeep into park and reaches over to unclip my seatbelt. He has me out of my seat and on his lap before I can protest.

"You listen to me, baby. I'm not using you as bait. I won't lose you and I won't put you in danger. I told you I'd protect you, and that's what I'm going to do."

"But, Noah, he'll come after me, even if you don't."

"No, he won't." He turns my face to his and kisses me hard. "I know you're not ready for this but you need to know, I love you and I'll do everything I can to protect you."

"How?" I ask dumbfounded. It's only been a week, how is this possible?

"I knew the moment I saw you, and now it's just compounded more and more. The thought of you being in danger makes me want to shoot everyone and take you far away from here."

"But, Noah—"

"Baby, I know you're not ready, so get back in your seat and let's go get a dog."

I spend the rest of the drive trying to work through all this. The thought of Noah getting hurt by Roy makes my heart clench, and maybe I do love him too.

We pull up to a large fenced in business and Noah pushes a call button.

"Yo, cuz, it's me, open up."

The gate opens and we pull through. There are several buildings, kennels with dogs, large obstacle courses, and people working with dogs everywhere.

I change into the regular glasses, making sure I keep myself protected, as Noah exits and walks around to my side of the jeep. I had already let my hair down earlier.

We walk through another gate and a man walks up to us. He's just barely taller than me, muscular, with dark brown hair and striking blue eyes. His face is covered in a scruffy shaggy beard and his hair is long and pushed back from his face.

I pull the hair band off my wrist and tie up my hair, not wanting it to get in the way.

"Hey, man, you UC again," Noah asks as they do the one-armed guy hug.

"Nah, just haven't shaved, been working with some new puppies. How you are liking the cold case division?"

"It's good. This is my girlfriend, Kenzie, I was telling you about. Kenzie, this is Jack Caine, my cousin."

"Hello," he says as he reaches out for me to shake his hand. I do and nod at him. "So, Noah says you're looking for a well-trained protective dog."

"That's what he said. I'm worried we work too much for a dog."

"Yeah, that can suck, but with his place you can train the dog to only go in one area and put in a doggy door, it will work. You'll need to walk it and take it for runs occasionally."

"Okay, what do you got?" I've never had a dog, I don't even know what I want in a dog.

"How about I take you and Noah into the kennel and we see who picks you. I believe a dog knows its owner."

I try not to laugh because it's just like Noah saying he knew I was his as soon as he saw me. He sees the smirk and leans down to whisper in my ear.

"Laugh it up, baby, and I'll spank that pretty little ass of yours."

I bite my lip to keep the chuckle in and to also maintain my composure because I want to jump him right here.

Jack leads us into a large kennel with lots of dogs. There are Rottweilers, pit bulls, German shepherds, big mastiffs, and other dogs I don't know. Most of them are running around but a few are just lying down looking around. Noah walks over to several shepherds and they come to him and sniff his hand.

"Come here, baby, let them smell you," he calls.

I'm about to walk over to him when a large whitish gray dog walks over to me and nudges my hand. I look at the dog. Its back almost comes to my waist in my heels. He's so big, I step back from him, but he drops his head and walks closer to me, pushing his head into my stomach.

"Um, Noah," I say as loud as I feel comfortable without scaring the giant of a dog.

He nuzzles into my stomach again and I finally rub his back. His hair feels coarse under my hand. He continues to push into me, and I feel off balance. I'm afraid to do it but I need to get over my fear if I'm going to have a dog, so I kneel down, and the dog stands taller than me. He lowers his face and licks my cheek. I giggle and he lies down in front of me. I stroke his back and he rolls over, putting his paws in the air, and I rub his belly.

"Who's a handsome good boy?" I coo at him, and he paws at my hand to pet him some more.

"Dude, I think your girl found her dog." Jack laughs.

I look over and Noah's watching me with awe on his face.

"Baby, do you know what that is?" he asks me.

I sit down on the grass, letting the dog rollover and lay his head across my lap. I pet his head and when I look at him, he calms me. His soft brown eyes look at me and I'm in love with him. He scared me at first because of his size, but he's just a gentle giant. His coat is mostly white but has gray around his ears and muzzle.

"I don't care what he is. Can we get him?" I look up and ask both of them.

"He's a one-year-old Irish wolfhound. I've trained him to protect, he'd be perfect for you."

"Really?"

"You're going to need to get a really big dog bed for him, but I'm pretty sure he won't let you leave without him." Jack laughs as the white dog wraps his paws around my legs and sticks his tongue out the side of his mouth.

"What's his name?"

"We speak Irish Gaelic to him. He was never going to make it as a police dog because he's too big, and I know Gaelic from my pa. His name is Bán, which means white."

"That's real original." I laugh and look at him. "Bán, do you want to come home with me?" I ask and he jumps up.

Noah comes over and helps me stand up and Bán steps between us.

"Oh no, you don't, boy, she was my girl first," Noah scolds the dog who just looks at him like he's crazy. "Okay, Jack, you got the list of things we'll need for him?"

"Yep, man, let me get it. I'm really glad he picked you, I was worried I was going to have to give him away to someone else because he just wouldn't take to anyone and I can't keep him here."

"I was scared at first, but he's so sweet and won me over." I confide in the guys.

We walk out of the kennel and Bán follows us out. Jack shows me commands and works with Bán and I for a while to make sure we are going to work out well.

After a bit Jack steps into one of the buildings and comes out with a large leather collar and thick leash.

"I had these made for him. He's a good dog and learns really quickly. I have a list of words here and a suggested app to learn how to pronounce the words, but if you use the combination of the Gaelic and English, he'll learn to recognize the words and learn English."

"Why did you teach him Gaelic?"

"Because I thought it was the right thing to do. He's Irish after all." Jack laughs and I fasten the thick leather collar with silver accents around his neck and clip the leash on.

Bán waits for me to move and then moves with me. I walk him to the jeep and open the back door, I pat the seat and he jumps up in it.

Noah comes over and opens my door for me and I get in and turn around to check on Bán. His butt is on the seat and his front paws are on the floor. I laugh, and when Noah gets in and looks, he laughs too.

We head back toward the city, stopping at a pet place to get our new dog some food, bowls, toys, a bed, and an extra-large two door dog door.

Bán walks around the pet place and people back up when they see how big he is. Some of the kids are scared of him because he's bigger than them. I know he won't hurt them, and I tell them they can pet him, and sure enough, he wins over most of the people in the store.

When we pull into the garage, Noah opens the back door but Bán won't get out until I come around and signal him to come to me. He jumps down and comes to my side. We step into the garden yard and I look at him.

"Go check it out, boy." He takes off, smelling everything, and I watch him.

After Noah takes Bán's new things into the house, he steps out and wraps his arms around me.

"Are you happy, baby?" He rests his head on my shoulder and we watch our dog as he runs around the yard.

"Yes, I am."

CHAPTER THIRTEEN

KENZIE

It's been a week and we've settled into a rhythm. Bán is perfect. We ended up rescheduling dinner with Noah's mom because he got called into work on Sunday.

Ballistics came back this week, and sure enough, all the bullets are a match. Roy shot all of them—Tommy and his grandmother, my brother, and Gino. They found Roy's DNA under Gino's nails, meaning the two men fought.

I've been officially placed in protective custody and my work told me to take a vacation. I spend my days gardening, working with my new dog, reading, and taking care of the men of the house. Zeke is still here, and there is talk he could be here for at least another month while the team he's on searches for a serial killer.

Today we are doing family dinner at Noah's mom's house and I can't bring Bán because he won't fit in the jeep with all of us. I hate leaving him and wonder how I'm going to when I have to go back to work. He's like my child.

"Ready, baby?" Noah asks from the patio and I turn to look at him from where I'm throwing the ball for Bán.

"Yep."

I'm in a bowknot backless sun dress in yellow with green and tan stilettos. This is a dress I bought right before Noah and I started dating and I haven't been able to wear it until now. I'm hoping it's not too sexy with the keyhole opening where the knot is.

Noah is dressed in jeans with a white button up shirt and a blue blazer. His brothers are dressed similarly. Their mother likes her Sundays to be nice dress instead of relaxing and it reminds me of being home.

I've been able to call and talk to my family but haven't been able to see them since the hospital. I miss them but don't want them in danger. I wish we could cancel this dinner, but Noah and Zeke assure me it's safe and that their mom is always protected.

Noah opens the back door of the jeep and I slide in behind the driver side. I don't pressure him to let me drive because I know how worried he is with my safety right now. I just pray they can catch Roy soon.

We pull up in front of a large white house with a glass door. The driveway has a couple other vehicles in it and one I recognize. Tears start and my door is opened, and Noah pulls me out.

"I wanted to surprise you, baby. Our families are having Sunday dinner together."

"But?" I can't say the words.

"It will be okay. Watch."

The door opens and a woman with dark brown hair steps out. She has full cheeks and is dressed elegantly. She doesn't look like she's almost fifty, her skin is still smooth.

She hugs Jericho and Zeke before she comes to me. Her blue eyes are so similar to Jericho's.

"Hello, Kenzie, I'm Gaia, welcome to the family." She takes me into her arms. A small Maltese dog is jumping at her feet, but the growl of a big dog has me looking around her. There is a large mastiff standing in the doorway.

"Apollo, heel," Zeke commands, and the dog comes to his side and quiets.

"When are you moving home so you can take that beast with you? He's eating me out of house and home," Gaia complains as she takes Noah into her arms. "Hello, Noah, you are looking happy." She smiles at him and I see all the boys in that smile.

She takes my hand and leads me into the house. My father and brothers are sitting on the sofa watching a game, and I tear up at the memories of them doing this every Sunday when I was growing up.

"Ahh, *bellissima,* I see you haven't decided to trade up and break it off with my nephew." Uncle Romeo jokes as he takes me in his arms and kisses both my cheeks.

Gaia and her brother look so much alike, even down to the shade of blue in their eyes. Noah pulls me back and scowls at his uncle who just laughs at him.

My brothers and father come over and meet the other Caine brothers. Marco knows Jericho from working fires together, and Enzo says he's heard about him. My mother walks out of the kitchen and takes me in for a hug, and I'm still flabbergasted that she doesn't hate me and that it feels like no time has passed at all. Her hugs feel the same as they did when I was a kid. I missed them so much.

When we all settle down to eat the big Italian feast, memories of doing this before makes me have to excuse myself. I head to the restroom and try to get myself under control. I don't want to ruin anyone's day and I know I will with my pain. A knock on the door has me turning.

"Just a moment." I pat my eyes with the towel and make sure I don't look like I was crying.

"Open the door, baby." Noah's voice comes through the door.

I walk over and let him in. He holds me close. When I start crying again, he leads me upstairs and into a room. I look around at all the hockey posters and know this was his room growing up. He walks over to the bed and sits down, pulling me down with him.

"Let it out."

"I don't want to ruin their day."

"You aren't, baby."

"How do you know?"

"Because they are all getting along and are just worried about you."

"Noah, I missed all these Sundays because I thought I was doing the right thing six years ago."

"If you had stayed, we might not have met."

His words hold the truth and I realize I had to leave. I had to run. In order to have this right here. This man and this moment. I lean forward and kiss him, he breaks it off before it gets too hot.

"Baby, not that I didn't dream about taking a sexy blonde in my bed, I don't want your family to hear you scream my name, it's bad enough my own brothers hear it. I want it all to myself. All of you."

He stands and we walk back downstairs to the table where I enjoy the rest of the meal.

As we are leaving after my family has already left, Gaia pulls me into her arms.

"I'm so happy for you and Noah. Call me if you need

anything. I know those boys are demanding and a handful sometimes."

"Oh, I only have to make them breakfast and they are nice to me."

She laughs. "None of them like to make that meal."

When we get home, Bán runs around my legs. Noah and I have trained him to sleep downstairs because I don't want to have sex in front of him, and Noah doesn't want to find out if Bán will attack him if he makes me scream. He already scratches at the door and whines when he hears us.

I'M WALKING around the parlor attached to the master suite, waiting for Noah to get done closing up downstairs and getting Bán settled. I like this room as is, but I don't see why we need a whole living room to ourselves. I know what I could imagine this room looking like. Noah is everything I've ever wanted in a man. He protects me. He cherishes me. He likes my family but doesn't let my brothers push him around.

I slide my hand across the back of the sofa that faces the fireplace, a large rug is on the floor too.

"What are you doing in here just walking around?"

Noah's voice startles me and I turn to see him leaning against the arched entrance into the room. When Noah remodeled, he kept the arches, leaving the beautiful lines. The architecture is breathtaking, but nothing like the man with his legs casually crossed, and his muscles straining against the material cut to perfection on his body. I tilt my head and smile at him.

"I like this room, but I want to change it."

"Yeah, baby, what do you want to change about it?" He smiles at me and I wonder if he knows what I'm thinking.

I bite my lip trying to decide how I'm going to work all this out. I've never seduced a man and I want to tell him what he needs to hear while we are making love.

"Well... Why do we need two living rooms?" I flirt as I slip my hand behind my back and release the low zipper. He stands straight and watches me carefully, his eyes devouring me.

Of course, he's a detective and figures out what I'm doing. So, before he can reach me, I let the dress slide off my shoulders and fall in a pool at my feet, leaving me in the yellow thong only as no bra could be worn under the dress. He stalks toward me and stops in front of me.

"You can decorate this room any way you want to. If you want to make it an office, you can. If you want to open the walls to every room, I'll do it," he says as he reaches out. His fingers trail from my shoulders down over my breasts and to my hips, where he pulls me to him fitting our bodies together. He leans down and kisses my neck, and I tilt my head to give him more to nibble.

"I was thinking it would make a perfect nursery." I sigh as he kisses and licks across my collarbone.

He pauses and pulls back, and looks down at me.

"What are you saying, baby?"

"I'm saying I want to be yours forever. I want to live here with you. I want our crazy families to come here on Sundays. I want to have your baby. I love you, Noah," I say as I pull him in closer.

He doesn't give me a moment, he takes my mouth in a hard kiss claiming it. Claiming me. He places his hands on the sides of my face and looks down at me with love in his eyes.

"I love you too, Kenzie Russo, and I want all those things with you too."

He releases my face and lifts me up, my legs wrap around his waist and he sits me on the back of the couch. He pushes into my body and I grab his shirt, ripping it open. He slips it off and wraps his arms around me and kisses me again. I turn my head to allow him to go deeper as I unhook his belt and then his jeans. I push them down his hips, along with his boxer briefs. Pulling back, I look up at him.

"I want you in me, now."

He growls and pulls me off the back of the sofa and rips my thong. He twists me around and hikes up one of my legs and I feel his cock at my entrance. Holding my waist with one hand and my hair in his other, he thrusts into my body. The sofa moves and he thrusts again and again, holding my body captive.

"Oh, Noah, I love you so much," I tell him again, and his thrusts become more erratic.

"Fuck, Kenzie, you're killing me here," he growls as he tips my hips using the hand on my waist.

"Noah, your cock feels so good. Please, deeper. I need you deeper, honey," I beg him.

I don't know where the words come from, but releasing the past and knowing he's going to be mine makes me want to give him all of me. All my desires. All my passion.

He pushes me forward, his hand still in my hair. I feel like I'm about to fall over the back of the couch, but he holds me so tight I trust him. He kicks my leg still on the floor, spreading me wider. With the angle and wider stance, I feel his cock hit that spot inside me and stars start to bloom behind my eyes. I'm so close and he's thrusting so hard the couch is now against the rug and stopped moving. He stops his thrusts and I cry out.

"No! Don't stop. I'm so close."

"Say it again, Kenzie," he growls.

"I love you, Noah. I love you."

He starts thrusting again, and this time he lets me go over. I tighten down on his cock and he groans as we both come together.

"I love you too, baby," he says on the last thrust as he holds our bodies together.

He pulls out, steps back and helps me stand normally, then spins me around. His mouth is on mine again.

When he pulls back, he smiles at me as he steps out of his jeans completely.

"I'm going to start the shower. You get out of those heels and meet me in there."

I look at the mess we made, clothes and buttons strewn everywhere. I look at the windows and realize we need to get curtains because people across the street could look through those blinds.

I meet him in the shower, where as usual, he makes love to me on the bench.

CHAPTER FOURTEEN

KENZIE

I sigh as I roll over in bed, remembering Noah waking me up earlier and making love to me before he got in the shower and left for work. I really need him to stop keeping me up so late so I can wake up earlier and make him breakfast. I also need to order some more groceries. I know I'm going to have to go back to work next week, I only have two weeks off, and this is the second week. Hopefully they can capture Roy in that time frame so I don't have to take any more time off.

I hear Bán's soft snores from the floor and look over the side of the bed. He's lying on the rug sleeping. Noah must have let him in the room before he left.

I smile because I'm completely by myself. Last week Jericho took some extra time off to hang out with me, he didn't want me by myself, but today it's just me in my home. Perfect.

I take a shower and get dressed in a pair of ripped up jeans and a tank top, and head downstairs. Making myself a single cup of coffee, I start my list of things I want to do for the day. I look out at the backyard and see the light sprinkle of rain. I hope it clears up so I can work in the garden. I've started a small vegetable and herb garden. In the winter I can transplant the herbs to come in the house.

I walk over to my laptop and open up the local grocer's website and order food for the next couple of weeks. I know it will take a couple hours before they can deliver, so I head downstairs and decide to clean down there now that none of the guys are home.

I've been down here for a while when Bán stands from his bed and looks at the stairs. Crap, I won't be able to have the delivery guy come in without Bán having an issue with him. He doesn't like strangers, we found that out last week when the mailman needed to drop off a package. If Jericho hadn't been here, Bán would have taken the mail carrier out. Jericho had to hold him back. I make a quick decision.

"Bán, suí fanacht," I order him to sit and stay using the Gaelic I've been learning, including the hand signals. "Bán, sit, stay," I order him again in English.

He sits on his bed and stays. I walk up the stairs and close the door to the basement as the doorbell buzzes. I look through both sets of doors and see the grocer's delivery guy and unarm the house. I open the first door and open the second to help him carry in all the groceries that are sitting on the step.

"Thank you. Let me help you."

I grab a couple of the bags and turn my back to him. I'm in the house and almost to the kitchen when I hear the gunshot. I turn quickly and scream when I see Roy step into my house. I run for the door to let Bán out, but his voice stops me.

"If you let that dog out, I'll kill him," he says as he points his gun at the delivery boy who lifts his head and shakes it at me, his eyes pleading with me to listen to Roy.

Bán is barking and scratching at the door. If I can just get to my purse, or get to the panel, I can get help or protect us all. I decide on my purse because I won't have to get past him.

I slowly back up to head for the dining room where I left my purse when we came in last night. If I could just get to my gun. Roy rushes me and grabs my face in his hand, squeezing my jaw tightly. I look into his pale brown eyes and see nothing but hate. His blond hair is cut short to his head and he has a beard covering his chin. But his eyes, I know those eyes.

I punch at his face. He doesn't expect it and the gun drops from his hand as his fist comes at me. I dodge the hit and he hits the wall, breaking the wood paneling. He grabs me again and slams me into the other wall. He pushes into me, bruising my chest. Grabbing up above his elbows, I slide my feet away from the wall to give myself more room and turn him using his arms and weight against himself. He slams into the wall and I hear a crack. I proceed to pull up my knee into his belly several times and turn to run for the dining room.

My hair is yanked back, and I scream as Roy throws me to the floor. I fall onto my back and he jumps on top of me and hits me in the face. I block the next hit and plant my feet as I twist, throwing him off my body. He hits the table and knocks over a chair.

"My queen has some fire now." He calls me by the name I hate, and I flip up and get on my feet.

He kicks out and knocks me back to the floor. I use my arms to keep me from smashing my face against the hardwood. He stands over me and I look up as he lifts a chair to hit me. I roll and feel the pain of the impact on my back, a spindle of the chair clatters to the floor. I turn my head in time to see him hold the chair up high and I wait, knowing what's coming next. As it comes down, I roll and slam into his legs before he can hit me again. The chair splinters apart and he tries to kick me away from him, but I wrap myself around his legs trying to bring him down to my level.

I reach up with my right arm and close my fist knowing the hit to his junk could drop him on me, but I need to get away from him. He hits my head and back. I hope my aim is good and I swing with everything I am, but he turns slightly at the last minute and my fist grazes his thigh before it hits his junk. He screams in pain and falls. I rise on my knees and punch him in the face a couple more times.

"I'm not your queen, fucker," I yell at him as I stand to my feet.

I scream in pain as he stabs the side of my thigh, leaving the knife partially in my leg. I chop at his arm to break his grip and yank out the knife. I throw it across the room and stumble back, trying to get him into a green zone and away from me.

I'm not quick enough and he sweeps my legs again, and I fall back and roll toward the patio doors. I'm past where my purse is but I can't think about that now. My whole body is burning. I crawl to the glass door and try to open it, but his fingers are in my hair again.

"I saw you last night." He slams my face into the glass door, at the last minute I turn so only my cheek impacts. "You are a fucking whore. I saw you. You are mine." He slams my face into the glass again, over and over.

I have no more energy to turn my head and pain radiates from my nose, my cheeks, and my forehead. He releases me and I fall to the floor with blood pooling around me.

"Now he's dead."

I hear the delivery boy scream, begging for his life, followed by the gunshot. I focus on Bán barking away and banging into the door.

"Fucking dog."

I hear a couple more gunshots and then quiet.

No! Not my dog. Oh God, not Bán. I try to rise up but my hands slip in the blood. He grabs my shoulder and rolls me over. Pain shoots through my arm.

"You should have never fucking left me."

The gun comes down and I feel the impact against my temple, and then nothing.

NOAH

Mandatory radio protocol training with handheld has to be done every few months and it's Linc's and my turn. The handheld on his desk squawks.

The ten codes for shots fired and possible kidnapping come across and we listen for a location. Something in my gut tells me this isn't going to be nothing, but instead something very important to me.

The dispatcher rattles off the address and I'm up and moving before she finishes. I hear Linc on his phone, but I don't care, that was my address.

I hear the unit tell dispatch they acknowledge the call. I grab my cell and dial Jericho. I don't give him a chance to speak.

"He's got her. Call Zeke and meet me at the house." I hang up as my phone goes off again and unknown number flashes across the screen. I answer it praying it's her and she's safe.

"Noah, he's got her. I called in police as soon as I figured it out," Bekah says breathlessly into the phone.

"What do you mean?" I can't understand.

"She had groceries delivered. I saw the kid, confirmed it wasn't Roy and stepped away for a moment while they were loading them into the house. When I came back and noticed the groceries were still on the stoop and the door was open, I pulled up the camera in the garden and saw him attacking her. I'm sorry, Noah. I'm tracking her now, but her bracelets aren't working."

"Call me when you have a location."

I hang up and try to get home as fast as I can. When we pull up there are police, ambulances, and fire everywhere. I see a body on a gurney being carried down the stairs. The sheet is covering their face and I yell as I run.

"No! Kenzie!" I rip the sheet from the face and see a young man I don't recognize. "My fiancée was in there." I pant, my hands going to my legs as I bend over, the pain in my chest almost too much to bear.

"There's no one else in there, Detective Caine. The house is clear," an officer says as he walks out.

"Our dog. Where is our dog?" I demand.

"A dog?" he asks, but I push past him and into the house.

I know I need to be careful and not trample evidence, but I need to find my girl and her dog. I step over blood puddles, broken pictures, holes in the wall, and shattered glass. I look around and see the basement door is closed. But I see the bullet holes.

"Mother fucker," I yell as I rip open the door.

Sitting at the bottom of the stairs is Bán shaking. I sit on the first step and he walks up to me with a limp. I look at the bullet holes and then at the dog. He has no marks on him except splinters of wood in his coat. He must have jumped down the stairs when the asshole started shooting at the door. I know Bán would have been barking to get to Kenzie if she made any noise he didn't like.

"Let me in, you fuckers." I hear Zeke yell and look around the wall to him.

"Get his leash. He's alive and limping, but I need to look for Kenzie."

Zeke hands me his leash and I look around for someone not doing something. Someone not busy. When I see a young cop just staring at the back-slider door, I yell at him.

"Hey, you come here and take my dog outside."

"Sorry, Detective Caine, you're going to need to keep him there. I don't want him trampling through my evidence." Detective Ryzer stops my plan.

Shit, I need to figure out where to put Bán so I can keep looking.

"Bán, bed," I command, and he walks down and sits on it. "Stay," I order, and he stays. I stand and close the door, shutting him in.

When I turn, Detective Ryzer has moved the uniformed cop and is looking at the glass door too. I join her and my body shudders at the image. There's a perfect imprint of Kenzie's face in the bloodied glass.

"Fuck, Paeton, is that what I think it is?" I ask the detective, using her first name. Kenzie fought hard.

"Yes, it is."

A woman stands next to my brother, she's over a foot shorter than him with light brown hair and green eyes.

"Detective Caine, I'm Special Agent Jamie O'Malley. I was with your brother Zeke when he got the call. If the FBI can be of any service, please let us know." She has a soft voice with a heavy southern accent.

"Thank you, ma'am." I brush her off and continue to

follow Detective Ryzer around. "Paeton, do you have anything?" I beg.

"Look, let me process the door, and if you carry your dog, you can take him out the back." She placates me.

I watch as she processes the back door and the perfect full handprint that had to be from Roy.

"We got him?" I ask her.

"Yes, we do, if this comes back to the prints we have on file for him. I'll run the print, but we already have his DNA and there's enough blood around here with witness statements that it was him."

I want to be happy with that knowledge but until I have her safe, I know he can still hurt her worse than he already has.

After Ryzer has photographed, collected, and fingerprinted the back door, she opens it and I go get Bán, lifting him carefully. As I step out the back door, my cell phone goes off, so I hand the leash to Jer knowing if I let Bán go he will try to get back into the house to look for Kenzie.

"Caine," I answer, praying someone has found her.

"We got her." Bekah's voice comes across the line. "She's in the Bronx in an abandoned warehouse. I got the address." She continues.

"Caine, you're going to want to get to her ASAP. She was unconscious from what we could tell from the security camera across the street that Bekah hacked into." A male voice comes across the line.

"Sorry, that's Derek, Noah. I've sent the address to your phone. I'll give you a bit of a lead before I call in backup for you," she answers the question I didn't ask.

"If we were closer, I'd offer to help. You could use a sniper, but all our operatives in the area are on another case. Bekah will track your cell."

They disconnect as my captain yells my name from the door. I'm standing by the waterfall feature in the garden and I try to relax as much as possible so I don't give any indication I know where she is. I want to end this, and I know they will pull me now.

"Caine, did you hear me?" he yells again, and I turn around.

"Sir?" I walk to him and make eye contact with Zeke, giving him an almost imperceptible nod, letting him know we found her.

"Caine, you didn't tell me you were dating a witness, or even a potential suspect on this case." He's right, I never did. I didn't want to be pulled from the case.

"Sir, she was never a suspect and she didn't witness anything, she's a victim." I clarify.

"Technicalities. You're off the case and this is now a matter for Main Division. Linc is catching them up now. Stand down."

"Yes, sir." I nod at him.

"You're taking this too good, Caine. If I find out you are holding back information, I will suspend you."

"Yes, sir."

I wait for him to turn around and head out of the house. I unclip my badge and set it on the table on the patio, along with my department issued gun after I remove the magazine and clear the chamber. I turn my back on the life I thought I always wanted and head for the life I need to protect, the woman I love with everything.

My brothers fall in step with me as I head for the garage. I open the gun safe I keep there and pull out both of my Springfield XD9s and a second holster. I slip one in the holster under my jacket where my service weapon usually goes, and the other into my back in the second holster.

Jericho reaches in and grabs the H&K P30, along with a Mossberg 12-gauge shotgun. I watch him put the small gun into the back of his cargo pants and dump several shotgun shells in his pockets. Zeke only reaches in and grabs a tall black case that I know holds his custom AR15.

"I got an address. Let's go," I say after I make sure we have three vests.

As I'm jumping into my jeep, the garage door opens and Linc, along with Special Agent O'Malley, walks in letting Bán in too.

"Zeke, open the back so he can go with us." I don't want to bring him with the limp, but I don't trust anyone to watch him and he could help us. I know Jack trained him to be a protection dog, along with tracking.

"Noah, do you really want to do this?" Linc asks me.

"It's not a choice, she's mine and I'll do anything to bring her home. If we call in a tactical unit, she could be dead before then."

"Okay. I'll give you a head start. Have Jericho text me when you get on scene and I'll have the cavalry roll," he says exactly what Bekah said, and I appreciate both of them allowing me to end this.

"Zeke, I'll clear you a path," O'Malley says as she turns away, but the look she gives him before she does says more than I expected.

As I back out of the garage, I look over at him and he just shakes his head at me. After this is all taken care of and I have my girl back, I will be sitting down with my brother and talking to him.

CHAPTER FIFTEEN

KENZIE

I come to feeling cold and wet. Everything hurts and I know I'm not where I should be. The images flash before my eyes of the fight and I jerk upright, my muscles all tensing in pain. Blood is still slowly dripping from my broken nose and the wound in my thigh.

"Well, well, well, it's about time you woke up, my queen," Roy says from behind me and I turn to look at him. He walks toward me and I crab crawl backwards, trying to get away from him. He grabs me by my hair and pulls me up into his face. "I wanted forever with you. You were supposed to be mine, but I see now that isn't going to ever happen. You're nothing but a whore." His gun hand swings out and I try to turn my head, but his grip tightens. I throw up my arm to block and pain explodes through my arm.

I'm not going to let him win. I've trained to protect myself. Pushing the pain out of my mind, I focus on getting loose. I remember the training. My hand goes to the top of his like I've been taught, and I swing a knuckle hit to the inside of the arm holding my hair, right up above his elbow. I bring my left knee up at the same time and nail him in the groin. He was too focused on what I did to his arm, hitting him in a nerve that caused him to let me go, and didn't cover the knee to the groin. He falls to the ground on his knees with his hands clutching his groin. I grab for the gun and put it to his forehead. His eyes widen in terror.

"I'm not your queen and I never was. Leave me alone." I step away from him. "You're not worth it."

I turn my back on him and limp to the door as it opens, and Noah is running in toward me. I'm so relieved to see him I don't think about anything but getting to him. The gunshot rings out from right behind me and I watch as Noah's body is knocked back from the force of the bullet hitting his vest. He falls into a shelving unit and things fall onto him as I scream his name.

"I'm not done with you, bitch." Roy grabs me from behind with one arm around my neck and the other holding a large .44 Magnum revolver to the side of my head.

"Noah," I beg, but he doesn't move.

"Drop the gun or I'll shoot him in the head," Roy grits out next to my ear.

I drop the gun as Roy drags me out the door Noah came through, and we come face-to-face with Jericho standing there with a shotgun. In the distance sirens can be heard.

"Drop your gun, asshole, and let her go," Jericho demands. "Police are just around the corner."

"Never," Roy says as he presses the gun to my head. "If I can't have her, no one will."

"Jericho, Noah's been shot, you need to get to him. Let me go," I beg.

"Shut up, bitch," Roy growls.

I'm not going to let Noah die because of me. Roy has

taken so much from me and it's all my fault for allowing him into my life. I start to struggle, not caring about the arm tightening across my neck. We are the same height, so I know no one is going to be able to shoot him with the current hold he has on me. I grab for his gun and pull it down as I jerk in his arms and flay my body around screaming at Jericho and the cops that have finally arrived.

"Shoot him," I beg, but no one listens to me.

Roy and I are struggling over the gun and I don't think, I just react. I wrap my fingers around the trigger. On a sigh, I look at Jericho.

"Tell him I love him."

I pull the trigger. The burn from the bullet going through my body and then out causes me to scream in pain. I fall forward and I hear two things. My name being screamed in agony and another gunshot followed by more. I lie there on the ground writhing in pain, glad it's over. I close my eyes ready to let go when two strong hands hold my face gently.

"Open your eyes, baby. Don't you leave me," Noah begs as I open my eyes and smile at him. He's safe.

"I love-" The pain so intense, I fall into oblivion.

NOAH

"Kenzie," I yell and scream as I hold her face trying to get her to return to me.

Jericho is working on her, putting pressure on the wounds. When her eyes fluttered closed, my heart seized in my chest. I can't lose her like this. Her face is swollen over the left side, her nose still dripping blood.

"I couldn't get a shot until she fell. I'm sorry, bro," Zeke apologizes for not shooting sooner, but as I came out the door, I saw the predicament and then the gun went off and I realized what she had done.

"Excuse us, we need to get her to the hospital right away." Another paramedic steps up.

I barely hear Jericho give his report on her condition and watch as they load her in the ambulance. I jump in behind them and they look at me.

"Sir?"

"I'm not leaving her side, she's my fiancée." It's only slightly a lie.

The ride to the hospital only takes moments, and when they wheel her out, they take her directly to an OR and I'm left waiting in the waiting room. A nurse shows me where I can clean up as my hands are covered in Kenzie's blood. When I come back out, Jericho and Zeke are standing waiting for me. The doors open and in walks Kenzie's family, along with my mom and uncle. Mom walks over and hugs me, not carrying about the dirt and blood on me. Kenzie's mom cries harder when she sees it. I turn as the OR waiting room door opens again and in walks Linc with my go-bag.

"Thanks, man. How did you know?"

"I saw you on scene. Jack has Bán and is taking him to a vet to have his leg checked out."

"Thank you."

I step out of the room and head back to where I was before to change into a pair of jeans and a T-shirt. When I return even more people are there—Trina and her husband, Paeton, and Special Agent O'Malley who is talking to Zeke in the corner. I watch her hand go up to his face and cup his cheek. He leans his head forward for a moment and bristles when he realizes I'm watching him, and he steps back.

I start pacing, trying to figure out where it all went wrong.

We pull up to the location and I look at Zeke.

"Find somewhere to take him down. If he comes out that door, I want him dead," I order him and he nods as he opens the passenger door, opens his case, and takes out his gun.

Zeke was an Army sniper and served six years before he joined DC Metro police. I watch him jog off.

"You stay here with that shotgun and watch too. I can't have you getting hurt. Keep an eye on Bán," I tell Jericho.

"Hey, I can shoot and fight just as well as you and Zeke," he argues.

"No. I need you here, she's going to need you to help her. You saw the blood, she's hurt. Please don't fight me on this." Dropping my head, I know I need to protect him from further involvement. Zeke is covered by the FBI, but Jer will lose his job. I already will be suspended if I'm not fired.

I approach the door from the side, not wanting to be surprised if Roy comes back out. The handle twists and I pray the door doesn't make any noise as I open it.

Only opening it a crack, I use the search mirror from my belt to look into the room. They are across the room fighting. I open the door slowly and slip in as I hear Kenzie tell him he's not worth it. She turns and sees me. I don't think, I just run to her. She's got blood dripping from her face and one of her eyes is starting to swell shut. She's limping and holding her arm. I hear the gun before I realize I wasn't keeping a close enough eye on Roy. I fall back into something metal and then nothing for a moment. I lie there trying to get my breathing under control and the feeling of nausea to subside. When I'm able to finally move, they are gone.

I stumble back to the door and open it, and my worst fears are confirmed. Roy has Kenzie by the neck with a gun to her, but she is struggling and screaming for the police and Jericho to shoot. I move toward them when the gunshot rings out and she falls to the ground. The bullet goes through her and into his chest, then another bullet rips through his skull and more bullets hit him. I stumble back, yelling for them to stop firing. I don't want Kenzie to get hit.

"Hey, buddy, you there?" A voice startles me from my thoughts. I'm staring out the window, but Marco is standing next to me. "Did you hear me?" he asks again.

"Yeah, sorry." I shake my head and try to focus on him.

"Your brothers told us everything, you did what you could. Roy was not going to give her up and she wasn't going to go back to him."

"That doesn't make me feel any better. I shouldn't have left her alone. I shouldn't have—"

"Family for Russo?" a nurse says from the door, and I turn to see a doctor walking up. He pulls a scrub cap off his head and waits for us to come around him. All of us.

"I'm Dr. Wright. Ms. Russo made it through surgery. The bullet tore through her upper left chest, missing her ribs and arteries. It did hit a vein that we had to repair. The bullet exited through her left scapula and hit a nerve there. We tried to repair what we could, but we will just have to see. She suffered from a knife wound to her right thigh that we closed up. Her other injuries consist of a nasal fracture, a zygomatic maxillary fracture, and an orbital fracture, all on the left side of her face." He pauses. "Sorry that's cheek, nose, and eye socket fractures. I had a plastic surgeon come in and help with repairing the damage. He inserted some plates and screws into the area around her eye and cheek. Her jaw wasn't fractured, so we didn't have to wire her closed, but she isn't going to want to move it very much for a bit due to the trauma. She sustained several deep tissue bruises all over her body. The biggest concern we have right now is the trauma to the frontal lobe of her brain. We understand her face was smashed several times into a glass window. There is moderate swelling in that area, and we are monitoring her for possible surgery to relieve the pressure. What I'm really trying to say is..." Again, he pauses and my heart seizes in my chest. I feel hands touching me and I realize I'm shaking from all the damage I couldn't prevent. "I'm sorry, I know this is a lot to take in, but the good news is she made it through surgery. The neurologist is monitoring her now, and while under sedation we did some neuro-monitoring and it looked promising. We have her intubated and ventilated right now. The next twenty-four hours will tell us more. We need her to wake up on her own. She never regained consciousness before surgery."

"She's strong, doctor," Sal says, and I nod my head.

"Can I see her?" I ask.

"Yes, they are moving her to the Neuro floor right now and once she is settled, they will come get you. Two people at a time though, Mr. Caine, I understand you are her fiancé, so we are going to allow you to stay up there. Maybe if she hears your voice she'll wake up."

"Thanks." I take a deep breath, trying not to let the tears out. "Thank you, sir." He shakes my hand and turns to leave.

My mother takes me in her arms and I do everything I can, but the tears start to seep from my eyes. I could still lose her, and I pray harder than I ever have. I can't lose her now.

After another thirty minutes, the nurse comes to get me and her parents first. I'm shocked by how fragile she looks in the bed.

She has tubes and monitors all over her. There's bandaging around her left shoulder and the side of her face. A sheet covers her from her waist down, her arms lying flat on the bed are covered in red marks and bruises along with

IV tubes. I notice white cloth cuffs around her wrists and will ask why she's restrained. There are tubes coming out from the bottom of the sheet for a catheter and for the pumps on her legs to prevent clots. Her hair is pushed back from her face in a hospital cap with small monitors all over the front of her forehead. She's got a ventilator attached to intubation tubes. Along with all the normal heart and breathing monitors too.

Her mother is barely through the door and crying. I walk over to the bed and notice a nurse sitting at a desk in the corner.

"Hello, I'm Karen and I'm here to monitor her. We have her arms restrained so she doesn't come awake and try to pull anything out before we can help her."

I just nod at the nurse and walk over to the bed. I carefully lean over Kenzie's right side and kiss her cheek.

"Baby, come back to me," I beg.

I walk around to her left side and gingerly take her hand in mine, letting her know I'm there. Her parents come over and kiss her and talk to her for a moment, then the next people come through. When everyone has had a chance to visit, Zeke steps back in.

"Jack called and said he'll keep Bán until she gets out. He's also going to see if he can bring him, that might help her. Jack said the vet told him Bán is good. The limp is probably from just a hard jump, but all the X-rays showed no damage. Jer and I are going to a hotel until they release the scene for us to go home."

"Thank you, Zeke."

"I'm sorry I couldn't shoot him sooner."

"It's my fault for not protecting her better."

"Both of you did everything you could. He was going to get her no matter what," Special Agent O'Malley says from behind Zeke. "As for a hotel, you can stay at my place. I have a spare room and the couch. They should be releasing your place tomorrow and then we'll get cleaners in there."

"Thank you, Special Agent O'Malley." I pause, not sure what else to say. She's helped keep my brother out of trouble for doing what he did in a different jurisdiction then he serves.

"Call me Jamie." She smiles. "Come on, asshole, let's get out of here." Zeke laces his fingers through hers and they walk out.

Again, I wonder what is going on with them. He's never mentioned her.

I pull a chair up and sit by my love holding her hand and quietly talking to her. The nurses come in throughout the night and check her monitors. One of them teaches me to disconnect her leg pumps and how to move her legs, pumping them back and forth. Her legs are covered in bruises and a stark white bandage that covers the knife wound on her thigh.

After two days I'm exhausted but I won't leave her side. My family brings me clothes to change into and I shower in the attached bathroom to her room. According to the CT scans, the swelling is decreasing but she still isn't waking up. The doctors said that because the swelling didn't increase in the first twenty-four hours, she will make it, but they caution us to the problems associated with extensive traumatic brain injuries and how she could have memory loss, personality changes, paralysis of her left side, and even issues with her sight because of where the swelling was.

I pray every chance I get. I ask my own father to protect her and bring her back to me. The reality of the situation hits me, and tears run down my face. I'm leaning over her right side where I kissed her cheek. I watch a tear fall from my face onto hers and watch as her cheek flinches. What the fuck, did that happen?

"Baby, are you there?" I ask her as the nurse on duty walks over to see what I did. I wipe the tear off her face and again her cheek flinches. "Kenzie, sweetie, come back to me," I beg.

"Mr. Caine, could you step back so I can check her?" the nurse asks, and I go to remove my hand from hers but she won't let me go. I look up at her eyes and they are open and panicked looking at me.

CHAPTER SIXTEEN

KENZIE

My body feels weighted down and I can't open my eyes. Every nerve ending hurts. Even my toes ache. I try to remember where I am and what's going on, but the pain in my head causes me to pause. I feel something wet on my face and I twitch my cheek trying to move it. My arms are too heavy and feel like they are pinned down. That's when I feel a weird sensation in my throat. It's like something is shoved down there. I want to choke and get whatever it is out, but when I try to tell my body to move, it doesn't.

A gentle brush of someone's fingers against my cheek has me twitching it again, and then I hear his voice. A deep rasp husky sound that causes tingles all over my body. He's here so I know I'm not in danger. But where are we?

"Kenzie, sweetie, come back to me." There's pain in his voice. Why?

Then a woman's voice "Mr. Caine, could you step back so I can check her?"

What is going on?

He tries to let go of my hand and that's when I feel straps holding me down. My eyes flash open and I can't talk, my body isn't moving like it should. He looks at me and I try to project the fear in my eyes.

"Baby." He pushes the woman in scrubs back and rests his hand against the right side of my face. My left side feels heavy and I can't move it.

I take a big breath through my nose and try not to panic. I try to raise my arms again. This time they move but stop. I'm strapped to the bed. I'm in a hospital. What happened to me?

I try to move my body around to escape. My legs are strapped into something that is squeezing them.

"Um." I try to talk and gag on a tube down my throat.

"Mr. Caine, go to the other side. I need to get her intubation tube out," the woman, a nurse, yells this time.

I watch her hit a button and all of the sudden my room is full of more nurses and doctors. Noah is pushed to the back and my eyes keep him in my sight. I can't stop looking at him. Something in my heart aches and makes this moment more important. I feel like I lost him, but he's right here and I can't explain it. Nurses and people step into my line of sight and try to block him from my view, but I move my head to see him again.

"Just look at me, baby, and stay calm," he says loudly, and he starts to move so that I can see him. When someone steps in that direction he moves again. I can't stop looking at him.

"Ms. Russo, I need you to cough," a man standing over me says, and I do. I feel scratching along my throat and then in my peripheral vision, I see a long tube. "Good job," he says as he steps back. "I'll let you talk to your fiancé and then we'll talk." I look at the doctor in question and everyone backs up as Noah steps closer to me.

"I thought I lost you. I thought you were gone forever," he says as he takes my hands after they're released from the binds.

"I...ck." I try to talk but only sounds like I'm croaking come from my mouth.

"Here, take a small sip." A nurse steps forward with a cup and I sip from the straw.

"I...d-don't...re-remember what ha-happened." My throat hurts and so does my jaw.

I reach up and feel bandages on the left side of my face. Tears start to roll down my face.

"I love you, baby. We'll get through this." Noah leans over and gently kisses my lips.

"I can see I should tell you what's going on." The doctor comes back over from where he was standing by the door. "You were shot and beaten, ma'am. You've sustained a traumatic brain injury from several blows to your head. You also sustained a knife wound to your right thigh."

"What?" My eyebrows shoot up and the pain in my head and cheek intensifies.

"Calm down, baby. Roy came to the house and attacked you. You fought him and while fighting over a gun with him, you were shot." Noah tries to explain.

"I do-don't remember that." I cry.

"Shhh, baby, rest. You're alive and that's all that counts." Noah's hands brush down my arms and I cringe as his hands rub across bruises. I look down at my body and see my knuckles battered along with my arms.

"A mirror," I beg, wanting to know why my face feels weird.

"Baby, maybe you should wait until the swelling goes down more." Noah tries to calm me again.

"Now, Noah. Now," I demand.

He looks over his shoulder and a nurse goes to get one.

"Ms. Russo, you've had surgery on your face to fix a broken nose, broken eye socket, and broken cheekbone." The doctor steps back into my line of sight. "There is significant swelling, but the plastic surgeon did amazing work."

This doesn't calm me. My eyes flash to Noah. I'm not vain but I don't want to be unrecognizable and I want to be beautiful for him.

When the nurse returns, I look in the mirror.

"Oh my God." I cry as I drop the mirror and pull my hands up to cover my face.

"Baby, you're just swollen right now. You're still beautiful to me. You fought—"

"Is he dead?" I grit out.

"You actually killed him, but Zeke finished him off for you, along with several cops."

"I shot him?"

"You did, baby. In the struggle for the gun, you pulled the trigger, shooting yourself. The bullet went through you and into his heart."

Something niggles in the back of my mind. Something important. I look around the room, none of my family or his are here. Family?

"Oh God, Bán!" I cry again and the sobs rack my body, causing pain through my shoulder, chest, and head.

"No, baby, Bán is okay," Noah says as he tries to wrap his arms around me.

"He is?" A vision hits me so hard pain shoots through my head again. "He was barking, and Roy shot the door where I'd put him. He stopped barking."

"You remember?"

"Just that." I lean back and my eyelids feel heavy and I can't stay awake. I fall into blackness.

"I'M NOT YOUR QUEEN, FUCKER," I yell at him as I stand to my feet.

I scream in pain as he stabs the side of my thigh, leaving the knife partially in my leg. I chop at his arm to break his grip and yank out the knife.

I come awake and sit up as fast as my aching body will let me. Noah is right there holding my hand, his other hand gently brushing down the right side of my face.

"I had a dream."

"It's okay, baby. I'm here and I'll never let anything else happen to you. I love you."

"I love you too, but you couldn't have stopped him. He would have killed you." Again there's that niggling in the back of my mind. "Did he shoot you?"

"Yes, got me in the vest." He looks shocked.

"I think I thought you were dead or dying. I just feel this overwhelming relief that you are here."

"I'm glad to be here too. Look." He lifts the T-shirt he's wearing, and I see the bruise over his sternum and left side of his chest where his heart is. I did almost lose him.

A thought hits me to something all the nurses and doctor said. "Did I forget you proposing to me?" I hope I didn't. I don't want to forget anything with him.

"Not yet, baby. I told them that so I could be with you and besides, it's going to happen as soon as we get out of here."

"Thank God, I don't want to forget that." I smile at him, and the pull in my cheek makes me cringe.

He leans forward and kisses my lips softly.

"Sleep, baby. I'm here and the family will come up tomorrow to see you."

I fall asleep feeling protected and loved.

IT'S BEEN a week since I woke up. I still don't have all my memories back, walking was difficult because of the stab wound and I'm a bit wobbly on my feet. My shoulder is healing, and the swelling has decreased from my face. All our family comes up and sees me every day, but not all at once. Noah stays by my side all the time and he's trying to talk the doctors into letting Jack bring up Bán, but the hospital administration is fighting him on it.

Today they are moving me to a normal floor. All my neurological testing pleased the doctors. I'm hoping they will let Noah wheel my chair out to the garden so I can see Bán. I'm also going to be starting physical and neurological therapy today.

I'M EXHAUSTED from the therapy, but I like the burn in my muscles from using them. I can't walk still without help because my left foot drags and I wear out too fast. Noah is pushing the wheelchair and heading for the garden just like I hoped. When the door opens, not only is Jack there with Bán, but so is Trina. I smile as best as I can with still having pain in my cheek.

Bán dances around when he sees me but one word from

Jack and he calms. As soon as Noah has my chair stopped and the brakes on, Jack leads him over to me. His large head lays on my lap and my heart calms from just rubbing his head. Tears start to fall and I'm so glad he's okay, but I could've lost him too.

"Is he hurting your leg, Keni?" Trina asks me in concern.

"No. I'm just so happy he's okay." I rub Bán's head and lean down to him, cooing and baby talking to him.

"You know your dog is kinda ugly?" Trina says seriously.

"No, he isn't, he's a very pretty regal boy." I defend him and she laughs at me.

"How much pain meds are you on, girl, 'cause his fur looks like he stuck his paw into a light socket?"

"He's an Irish wolfhound. This is what they look like."

"Kenzie, I had the vet do a complete check on him and he's doing perfectly well. I've been working with him on some new training to help you around the house," Jack interrupts Trina's and my bickering.

"Thank you, Jack."

"That's what family is for, sweetie." He leans over and kisses the top of my head. I watch as he steps back and sits next to Noah on the bench.

Trina and I talk and catch up on work gossip. She tells me about her first doctor's appointment, and I visit with her while I pet Bán, enjoying him being with me again.

"How long is your suspension?" I overhear Jack question Noah, and ignore what Trina is saying because I didn't know he was suspended. He told me he would take whatever time I needed him to take off.

"Four weeks total, but I only have three more weeks to go."

"Are you going back?"

"Yeah, but I'm talking to a company named Securities

International too. They've decided to open a New York office and want me to work for them. They offered me the chance to head it, but I'm not sure. I've gotta decide before the suspension is over."

Noah looks over and sees me looking at him.

"Um, Keni, I'll let you get some rest," Trina says as she leans over to hug me, but I'm still focused on Noah. Why didn't he tell me? Why did he lie?

"*Bán teacht*," Jack tells Bán to come to him. He looks up at me and I can see he doesn't want to leave me.

"Go, boy. I'll be home soon." I pat his head and he walks to Jack.

"We'll see you the day after tomorrow so you can start working with Bán on tasks you'll need him to do. We'll be at your therapy session."

"Really?"

"Yep. See you both."

An uncomfortable silence settles between Noah and me once we're alone.

"Why didn't you tell me?"

"I didn't want you to worry."

"Why did you get suspended?"

"Because I came to get you instead of letting SWAT come after you."

"With everything that has happened, I'm glad you came for me. Roy wouldn't have let me go. But you need to tell me everything from now on."

"Okay, baby."

"What's this job offer?"

"I'd be working for a security company investigating, protecting, doing some contract work within the US for the CIA since they can't, and with the FBI as needed."

"Do you want to do that?"

"I always wanted to be a cop until the moment I realized my hands were tied and I couldn't help you if I stayed being a cop. I knew Roy wouldn't go down without a fight, and I didn't want you to get hurt. Look at what happened to you when I came for you."

"Noah, I'm going to live. I might not be able to work as a dispatcher anymore, but at least I'm alive."

"Come on, baby, let's get you in your room before you fall asleep in your chair."

NOAH

Five days after she started physical therapy, my baby is able to go home. She has to use a walker to move around and has a wheelchair just in case. I pull up to the front of the house and look over at her. Even though all her memories haven't returned, I can see that something is bothering her because she's breathing fast and wringing her hands. She has nightmares and sometimes with them she remembers, other times she doesn't.

"Baby, you're safe. Bán won't be locked up anymore, regardless of who's at the door. You won't be alone for a while, and Roy is dead."

"I feel like I thought I was never going to be back here. I'm scared."

"If you want to move, we'll leave right now, and you will never have to see this place again." I swear to her and I will do it. I will do anything to help ease her.

"No. No, that's not it. I'm scared." Her eyes drop. "I'm scared I'll never remember."

"It's okay if you don't."

I turn off the jeep and jump out. As I open her door, the front door opens.

"Thank God you're home, dollface, I was getting bored with Jericho," Zeke says as he walks up.

She smiles at him and he goes to the back to get out her bags and things. I lift her out and carry her into the house.

"Where do you want to go first?"

"Um, how about the living room?"

"Okay." I kiss her as I turn right into the room.

I sit her on the soft leather sofa as Zeke sets her walker close by. Bán comes bounding into the room. He and Kenzie have been working together and he actually helps let her know when she's getting too tired to do things and her leg starts dragging.

I don't know what kind of training my cousin did on him, but he's been wonderful for her. She feels better moving around with him and he stays by her side. I watch as she pets him and loves on him.

"I have lasagna for my *bellissima*." Uncle Romeo steps through from the kitchen and walks over to kiss her hand.

"Yummy, the nurses were jealous every time you brought me food from the restaurant, or had one of your drivers bring me some."

I stand back and watch everyone and try to hold back from proposing to her right now. I told her I wanted her healed before I did that, but all I want is her to fully be mine.

IN THE TWO weeks since we've been home, I've watched her heal more. She's going to be in therapy for several more months, and now she's seeing a counselor to help with the panic attacks and nightmares.

After lots of consideration, I decided to take the job with

Securities International as the New York branch manager. I'll be in charge of hiring the new team and managing them from here, along with helping if the main office team has to come here.

I thought I would always be a cop but after everything that happened with Kenzie, I realized I want to be able to spend more time with my family and I want to be able to make a bigger impact on the world. Kenzie was upset with me at first, but I explained I'll only be on a part-time schedule until the office is up and running.

Bekah ended up having her baby almost two weeks ago, a little boy. One of my new bosses had triplets two months ago, and the other's wife had a little girl last week, so it will be another week before someone shows up to finalize my hiring. Until then I have plenty of vacation time owed to me from the NYPD and money in savings.

Jamie had the house not only cleaned, but repaired. The bullet holes were covered, and the paneling all repaired before Kenzie came home to it. It doesn't even look like anything ever happened in here.

Tonight, I've cleared out my brothers. Had a nice dinner delivered, and candles and water in wine glasses on the table. Because of the meds Kenzie is still on, she can't drink yet, and I know she wants a glass of wine badly.

"What smells so good?" Kenzie says from the doorway. "Oh my God, what did you do?" She smiles at me and I notice she isn't using her walker. She's in her short shorts and a tank top, and I know her bikini is on under it because she was laying out on the lounger in the sun earlier.

"Have a seat, beauty." I pull out her chair and she takes a seat as I carefully push the chair back in.

"I have all your favorites." I sit her plate in front of her and she laughs at me.

"What's the occasion?"

"Can't a man spoil his woman?"

"Yes."

As we eat, I think about the fact I'm going to get to do this with this woman for the rest of my life. After desert, I carry her upstairs and carefully sit her on the bed. We haven't been able to make love since before the shooting and I know the doctors told her today she could as long as we didn't put any strain on her shoulder or any of her other injuries.

I step back from her and lift my shirt over my head and unbutton my jeans and let them fall to the floor. I watch her eyes as they flare with desire. She reaches down and pulls her shirt over her head. I step into her space and reach behind her to unhook the stripped bikini top, and slide my hands down her shoulders, taking the straps down her arms. Leaning over her, I push her back on the bed.

"Climb up, baby." My voice comes across as a growl because of the desire and need.

I watch her shimmy up the bed. When her waist is in my sight, I lean over and kiss her belly before I unsnap her shorts and drag them off as she continues up the bed. I leave her in only the little bikini bottoms that match the top and show off her tattoos.

My mouth waters to have a taste of her, so when she is up against the pillows, I lower my head to her core and take in the smell of her desire. I pull the bikini to the side and lick up through her folds. Her hips buck off the bed and I rise up, pulling the bottoms off her before I settle in and hold her down as I take her like a starved man.

I straighten my tongue and fuck her with it, wanting to bury myself in her but wanting to make it good for her. Her hands are in my hair, pulling it as I take her clit between my lips and suck on it hard. I enter her with two fingers and find her G-spot. I rub it and her legs come up to my ears as she screams and orgasms.

I move up her body and line up my cock and thrust into her. I hold myself as we both calm down. I reach under my pillow and grab the little velvet box holding her ring. With my cock planted to my balls inside her, I lean up.

"Marry me, baby." It's not a question.

"Yes," she says as she writhes around under me.

"I mean it, Kenzie. Marry me."

She stops and looks at me as I slide the ring on her finger.

"Oh God. Yes."

I plant my elbows next to her head and proceed to work myself in and out of her, showing her what she does to me. When we come together, it's with "I love you" on our lips.

EPILOGUE

5 YEARS LATER

KENZIE

"**D**adda. Dadda. Dadda." Our youngest squeals from his playpen on the patio.

Lucas is two and the pride of his father. He's a spitting image of the Caine men with his dark brown hair and hazel eyes. The doctors were shocked by his over nine-pound birth weight. I wasn't, though, because I carried him and kept telling Noah he was too big.

"Daddy, Momma, give me my own garden." Kathleen our now four-year-old runs up to him rubbing her dirty hands on his slacks.

She was conceived the night Noah proposed to me. I was pregnant for our wedding and mad because I wanted to wait and wear the pretty gown, but he insisted that his kid was going to be born to married parents.

Noah leans over and picks up Lucas and sets him down so he can toddle around the garden. We love our house and have had to do some rearranging now that Jericho doesn't live with us anymore.

I was never able to return to work due to nerve damage in my hand from my shoulder, and I still have problem with my foot dragging if I get too tired. I finally remembered everything one day when I was sitting in the garden. I looked through the glass doors and it was like watching a movie. I wasn't a part of it but I saw it all happen before my eyes. I no longer have issues with panic attacks and Bán has been a constant in my life. He calms me and protects me. He's protective of the kids, right now he's following behind Lucas making sure he doesn't fall.

Noah still works for Securities International and there were a couple tough years, but he's made sure to always protect our family.

All our family still has monthly Sunday dinners together, we rotate whose house it's going to be at.

"How's my little momma?" Noah finally makes it over to me and helps me up from my kneeling position.

His hands rub my large belly. This is the last time he gets me pregnant is what I told him, but he laughs it off. He constantly tells me how beautiful I am pregnant, but with twins this time I'm ready to be done.

"I'm tired and your boys think it's a good idea to tap dance on my bladder while they fight for room in here." I hold his hand to my belly.

Yep, twin boys. Adam and Asher are due in four weeks, but the doctor said they could come in two weeks.

"Uncle Romeo sent us basanga, Daddy." Kathleen pulls on his pant leg again.

"Basanga. Momma loves his basanga." He leans down to pick her up.

"I knows, that's what I told him when he comes over."

"Baby, it's when he came over." I correct her.

"I said that." She rolls her eyes and her blond curls bounce around her face.

My daughter is the perfect mix of both of us. She has my blond curly hair, and a mixture of Noah's and my eye color with her hazel blue-gray eyes.

Noah holds out his hand to help me walk across the yard and back into the house so we can finish dinner before bed times. He lets my hand go just before the patio and turns to chase down Lucas. He lifts Kathleen onto his shoulders and tells her to hold on while he bends over to swing Lucas into his arms.

He still stops my blood and gives me tingles. He works out every day and at thirty-three, he has the young girls at the restaurant trying to pick him up. Leaving the police force didn't stop him from keeping his muscle and grueling workouts.

"Come on, momma." He smacks my ass as he walks by and the kids laugh at him, cheering him on.

I wouldn't change anything about my life.

EPILOGUE

15 YEARS LATER

NOAH

"Who the hell is she on the phone with?" I growl at my twin boys.

"I don't know, Dad." Asher ignores me as he plays on his phone.

"Lucas, sneak up there and find out who is making her giggle like that," I command my oldest son.

"Um, Dad, she's nineteen. Besides, I have a date. See you later." He slips out the front door and I growl.

"She's talking to some guy named Owen." Adam supplies.

"What?" I bellow. "He's like twenty."

"Calm down, papa bear, she's nineteen and it's okay." My beautiful wife's soft lilting voice comes from the laundry room.

I turn to look at her and even at forty-four and after four kids, she makes my blood run hot. I have to adjust myself because I want to take her upstairs and make her scream my name still. Then I remember my baby girl is on the phone with a colleague of mine.

Owen is the son of two of my co-workers in Scotland. He just got into town a couple days ago to do some work out of the New York office. Kathleen just finished her freshman year at Columbia University where she is studying biological science; she says she wants to get her PhD in microbiology and immunology or do something with neurology. She's always felt there was more they could have done for her mother, but Kenzie and I never felt cheated.

"When did they meet?" I ask the room.

"She met him when he came over the other day to drop off some paperwork for you, but you were at the restaurant doing something."

We lost my uncle last year to a heart attack, and since then, all of us have been keeping the restaurant going. My mom took over ownership but all of us help with management. Even Kenzie's brothers help.

"What paperwork?"

"I gave it you that day. I don't know what it was."

Then I remember what paperwork it was and I smile. It's tickets for the whole family to go to Scotland for a vacation and for my family to finally see the main headquarters for the company. We've traveled but never to Scotland. I've taken Kenzie back to Hawaii several times and to Europe with me on work trips, but we just never made it to Securities International's main headquarters. Kenzie has always wanted to go there and now she will.

I also have the surprise that she and I are leaving the kids with family and we're going to Italy for two weeks together before Scotland. I can't wait for it to just be us again for a little bit. I love our children, but between hockey, football, school, and every other activity our kids are involved in, I need some alone time with my wife.

"Adam, sneak up there and see if she's still on the phone." I point at Adam, who like his older brother, has my dark hair but both twins have their mother's beautiful gray eyes.

Both the twins stand at five foot seven at only fourteen and Lucas is just over six foot. They will all be tall and maybe taller than me. Asher has my bulk already, but Adam and Lucas are still on the thinner side like Jericho was at those ages. My beautiful daughter is five foot nine with long legs like her mother, and just like her, she tends to want to wear the tight jeans or short shorts.

"Hey, get out of here." I hear Kathleen yell and can't help but chuckle.

"Dad told me to." Adam throws me under the bus.

"Daddy, you promised," she yells down the stairs at me.

She moved into the top floor saying she needed privacy, but over my dead body is she going to bring boys back here. Between me and her brothers, we made sure that all her dates through high school knew they could go missing if they stepped out of line with her.

"Baby girl, I can't help myself," I holler back.

"Okay, enough yelling in the house," Kenzie says from the kitchen.

I head toward her and when I step into the kitchen, I see her in front of the stove making dinner. She's barefoot, cooking in our kitchen. I walk up behind her and wrap my arms around her.

"Baby, you know what I'm thinking right now." I press my erection into her still tight ass. Even with her leg issues, she still practices martial arts and works out.

"No, I'm not getting pregnant again, I'm too old for that."

"Oh, come on. You would look hot and sexy round with my baby."

"I've already done that three times to give you four kids. Nope, no more." She leans back after she puts the spoon on the rest next to the stove. "But we could always practice." She teases as she looks up at me. And I lean in and take her lips.

My dad was right about it all. I saw her and knew she was mine. My soul still sings Barry White for her.

SNEAK PEAK

ZEKE'S CHOICE

Mistake or Eternal Love?

When a weekend away to blow off steam ends up with matrimony Jamie doesn't know what to do. She can't get him to file the divorce papers and she won't either. Something about him soothes her soul.

Mistake. Divorce. Oh hell no. Zeke Caine won't admit either of those when it comes to Jamie. She's his and he can't let her go. Okay maybe he should have told his family.

Now they find themselves on the same task force after a serial killer. When a twist of fate puts Jamie in danger Zeke will kill anyone in his path to protect her. But is he ready to admit he loves her? Or is Jamie ready run and leave him behind?

Caine and Graco Saga

ACKNOWLEDGMENTS

Here we go again; this is where I thank everyone that has helped me with this book. I know most of you will stop reading right here but I want those that helped me to know how I feel. I sometimes don't say out loud what is in my heart.

First always to my family. Can you believe my 9th book is published? I can't believe you all put up with my crazy and even help me along the way. I love you all thank you!!

Paige, my girl Kenzie wouldn't be who she is without you. She is a lot of you and thank you for giving me a chance to write about what you do. Hope I did it right!

Dani, my senior going on full grown woman, thank you for helping me with all the music for this book and then others. I love hearing about your stories and can't wait to help you publish them.

Turdbutt, please don't be mad at me for the elements of

Kenzie that I know you will recognize. This is my therapy. I miss you every day and can't wait for you to decide to be a part of our lives again. We love you very much.

To my silent partner, girl I'm so glad you're a part of my life. Thank you for kicking my butt when I need and for being there when I need you.

Hall's what can I say that I haven't said before. Thank you for sharing your son with my family and for making my daughter feel so loved. Love you all!!

To the Adams family, we need to get together again and talk knives Shane. Chris you're the best sister a girl could have even when you're mad at me.

To all my family those that are blood and those that are heart. Love you all and thank you!

To my PA Mikki, thank you for helping when I was down and lifting me up. I appreciate your help every day.

Holy Shit Leah! This is one of my favorite covers. Thank you for the logos and all the help making the Caine & Graco Saga look amazing.

As always to my irreplaceable editor, Nadine, how do you keep up with me? You know my words and what I'm trying to say. I don't know where I would be without your guidance and help. Fight the fight lady you're a hero in my book.

To you the reader, without you I'm wouldn't be here. I look

forward to meeting all of you at different signings in the coming years.

To all the authors who've helped me, man I don't know what I would do without you. Thank you to all of you for shares, swaps, takeovers, advice and just support.

If I forgot you, I'm so sorry. Thank you!

Finally, to the one person that deserves more than my thanks. After 20 years of marriage you deserve everything. I love you honey! You're my number one fan, biggest critic and biggest supporter too.

ABOUT THE AUTHOR

Writer, wife and mother of three girls. E.M. Shue likes her whiskey Irish, her chocolate dark and her hockey hard hitting. She is an avid reader and you can find her Kindle packed full of all sub-genres of romance. When she isn't writing action-adventure, suspense, and strong woman she's spending time with her husband and youngest daughter that still lives at home.

She's currently writing the hot and steamy romantic suspense series Securities International and the novella series The Caine & Graco Saga. Her first two books in the Securities International series have both won the Colorado RWA Beverley contest, Sniper's Kiss in 2018 for Suspense, and Angel's Kiss in 2019 for Contemporary.

E.M.'s favorite saying is don't piss her off she'll write you into a book and kill you off in a new and gory way.

Made in the
USA
Columbia, SC